Sheep's Clothing

Sheep's Clothing

CELIA DALE

Thorndike Press • Thorndike, Maine

Library of Congress Cataloging in Publication Data:

Dale, Celia.
  Sheep's clothing / Celia Dale.
  p.   cm.
  ISBN 0-89621-912-7 (alk. paper : lg. print)
  1. Large type books. I. Title.
[PR6054.A38S5   1989]   89-33703
823'.914--dc20   CIP

Large Print edition available in the United States by arrangement with Doubleday & Company.

Cover design by Peter Eldredge.

Sheep's Clothing

Part One

1

Two women stood outside in the shadow of the overhang from the walkway above, for Mrs. Davies lived on the ground floor of a block of council flats: a mixed blessing, for although it meant she had no stairs to cope with and need never worry whether the lift had been put out of order yet again, she was a sitting target for hit-and-run bell-ringers, letter-box rattlers, window-bangers and dog dirt. And worse. So far she had been lucky, but she knew better than not to keep her door on the chain.

The older of the two women spoke: "Good afternoon, dear."

"Yes?"

"We're from the Social Services."

"Yes?"

"May we come in for a moment?" She was a pleasant-spoken woman in late middle-age, carrying an official looking briefcase as well as a handbag, from which she produced a plastic-covered card with her picture on it. She showed this to Mrs. Davies, who could just make out the likeness in the bad light of the overhang and through the narrow opening of the door.

"Just a minute, just a minute." Flustered, she closed the door and slipped off the chain, then opened it again. "The Social Services, is it? What do they want?"

"Nothing to worry about, dear. In fact, quite the reverse. Good news, we think you'll find."

"Good news? Is it me allowances?"

"Something like that."

"Well, you'd better come in."

"Thank you." Smiling, the woman stepped inside. Mrs. Davies made her way back into the sitting-room, where Radio 2 still sniggered away in its corner. The two women followed her, the second much younger than the first, a pallid girl with long brown hair reminiscent of the late John Lennon's, and carrying a zipped-up tote bag.

The older woman said, "This is my colleague, Mary. I'm Mrs. Black from the DHSS, group OAP B22 — that's a special group you won't have had dealings with before, which is why we're here. May we sit down?"

Mrs. Davies dropped into her own chair and the others sat on the hard chairs by the table. Radio 2's announcer said it was three o'clock.

Mrs. Black looked round the room. "What

a nice place you have here. Really cosy. Have you been here long?"

"Since they was built. He had his disability, see, from the war. We was one of the first."

"You must have seen some changes."

"Changes? You wouldn't believe! When me and Mr. Davies moved in, there wasn't a tree nor a blade of grass. All builders' rubble it was and the plaster hardly dried out. Still, we was glad to get here. Bombed out me and the boy was, while my hubby was serving. In the Middle East, he was, Alamein, all that, Italy. Then right at the end he got his disability. Crossing the Rhine, that was. Months he was in hospital. He never got over it, not really."

"Is this him?" Mrs. Black rose and picked up a photograph frame from the mantelpiece. A bright, terrier-faced man with a forage cap acutely angled over large ears looked back at her.

Mrs. Davies eased forward in her chair. "That's right. And that's the boy." She pointed to another frame from which much the same terrier face regarded her, but bareheaded.

"He's like his dad." She replaced the picture.

"They all say that. I never saw it myself."

"Does he live nearby?"

"No. Wolverhampton. He's in electricals, married with three kiddies. There's pictures in me bedroom."

"I'd love to see them. Mary, would you . . . that's if you don't mind, Mrs. . . . ?" She rustled apologetically among the papers in the brief-case.

"Davies, dear, Mrs. Annie Davies."

"Of course. Here we are." She drew an of-ficial-looking form from the folder.

"You go and get them, dear — in me bed-room, by me bed."

Mary got up and went out of the room.

"So you're all alone now?" Mrs. Black sighed. "It's hard, isn't it? I'm a widow my-self, twelve years it is now. You never get used to it. Still, I expect you've plenty of friends, living here so long."

"I did have. But most of them's passed away. They're a funny lot live here now, not like the old days. Then it was all neighbourly, help each other out; now most of them wouldn't hardly give you the time of day. All sorts, we've got now. I never go out after dark, spe-cially wintertime. Keep me door locked."

"Very wise, dear. It's only common sense these days."

Mary came back with the photographs. Mrs. Black studied them, smiling. "Oh, very nice, dear — what a lovely family! The little girl's

12

the image of you, isn't she, and what lovely hair. You must be proud. I expect they visit you, do they?"

Mrs. Davies's faded eyes filled and a tear or two rolled slowly into the pouches beneath. "Easter two years ago, it was. He can't spare the time, and now with the price of petrol. . . . He writes, though. He always writes for me birthday, sends me a card. I've kept them all; they're in that old toffee tin, dear, if you'd like to see."

Mary got up again and brought the tin, and they studied the cards and the old snapshots and the bunch of squashed artificial flowers from the hat Mrs. Davies had worn for the boy's wedding and the In Memoriam notices she'd put in the local newspaper each year for a time after Mr. Davies passed away and the brooch her gran had left her and a pair of shoe buckles; she didn't know where they'd come from but they were pretty, with sparkling stones, although no one wore things like that nowadays.

"You could get a few bob for those, dear," said Mrs. Black, turning them to and fro so that their paste caught the light.

"I daresay. But I'd not want to sell them, not just for a pound or two. It wouldn't be right."

"Well, that reminds me." Mrs. Black put

them back in the toffee tin and shut the lid briskly. "We mustn't waste any more of your time, Mrs. Davies dear. And we've other calls to make. Let's get down to business."

Mrs. Davies looked apprehensive.

"Now I told you it was good news, didn't I? I just need you to fill me in with a few details. Let's see . . ." She opened the briefcase and spread the papers it held over the table. "Now you're in receipt of the ordinary retirement pension, right? And supplementary, right? To the sum of — how much?" Mrs. Davies told her. "Right. Now because of your husband's disability it seems they've been underpaying you since six months after he passed away."

Mrs. Davies gaped.

"Yes, dear. You wouldn't credit it, would you, all those hundreds of clerks and files and computers and I don't know what-all, and they can make a mistake like that. Now he passed away when?"

"October 1976 it was. He was in hospital from the March."

She consulted the documents. "That's right. October. So it's due from April 1977. That's ten years due, Mrs. Davies."

"Well I never!"

Mrs. Black beamed. "I told you, didn't I? It's ever so nice when we're able to bring good news like that. People think the poor old DHSS is just for probing into people's business and hasn't got no heart, but I tell you, dear, we do care, especially workers like me and Mary in OAP B22. It's a specially caring department, isn't it, Mary?"

Mary spoke for the first time. "That's right."

"I wonder . . ." Mrs. Black paused. "I wonder if we could celebrate with a cup of tea? To tell you the truth, I'm parched."

Mrs. Davies surged in her chair, but Mrs. Black laid a hand on her arm. "No, you stay right there, dear, don't you stir. Mary'll make it, won't you, Mary, if you just tell her where everything is. The kitchen's through there?"

"It's in a bit of a pickle. I wasn't expecting . . . The tea's in the caddy on the shelf, the Coronation caddy . . . the sugar, the milk . . ."

"She'll find them. You just sit and let us give you a treat."

"You're ever so kind . . ."

"My pleasure," said Mary, and went out to the kitchen.

While she was gone, Mrs. Black encouraged Mrs. Davies to talk about her life. She knew from many years' experience that if old people had not withdrawn into a carapace of silence, as some did, then their prime need was to talk, to reach back into the past when everyone

15

was alive and kicking, and relive in speech the days when their bodies were vigorous, fulfilling all demands, and had not become merely a creaking case housing a still active memory. When Mary came back with the tea tray Mrs. Davies was in full spate and made no demur when Mrs. Black poured the tea and handed her a cup.

"I've put sugar in, dear, was that right?"

Mrs. Davies nodded, pausing only to sip the strong sweet brew, for she was describing a holiday she and her husband had taken just before the war, not long married and long before they had the boy, and they'd gone to the Hippodrome and seen Gracie Fields and waited at the stage door afterwards to get her autograph. And she'd got it somewhere still, and the programme. It was Coronation year, the tea caddy reminded her, King George VI, that was. She and her friend May had stayed out all night on the pavement in Whitehall just by the Cenotaph, thousands of them, all having singsongs, jolly as anything. Her hubby wouldn't come, didn't hold with royalty, although he joined the forces soon enough when old Adolf started up, well, that was different, wasn't it. She and May had seen all the processions as close as close, and the King with his crown on his head looking ever so peaky although she was lovely, smiling and waving away just the way she does now, that lovely smile. . . .

When two cups had been drunk and the teapot was dry, Mrs. Black gently checked the flow and brought Mrs. Davies back to the purpose of their visit. She explained in detail the ramifications of employment stamps (as they had been in those days) and Mr. Davies's dues, his disability and the consequent benefits to which he had been entitled, although, due to a failure in another departmental group, OAP B551A, the Davieses had never received this: so although Mrs. Davies had been drawing her own supplementary (but only recently, when the cost of living had risen so sharply and her retirement entitlement, see leaflet NP32, proved inadequate), she was nevertheless subject to full entitlement for disability payments retrospective to 1977 at full weekly rates until April 1979 and thereafter half rates up to and including April 1987, after which her case would come up for review both by group OAP B22 and the negligent OAP B551A, and Mrs. Davies was therefore in the happy position of entitlement to a tidy sum.

Mrs. Davies was dazed. She lay back in her chair, cheeks flushed, breathing heavily, and in a blurred voice asked: "How much?"

Mrs. Black did some sums. "Well, dear, at a quick estimate I'd say that twelve months at twelve pounds thirty-eight, and that's from '77 to '79, and then six pounds seventeen approximately thereafter, that's from '79 to the financial year April '87, I should reckon that's just about — well, I've not got my calculator with me, but I'd say it'll see you the better for quite a few hundred pounds."

"Hundreds!" Mrs. Davies gasped. She sounded drunk, and indeed her lids were closing over eyes that showed an astonished joy fast dimming into sleep.

"Hundreds," said Mrs. Black firmly.

Mrs. Davies half smiled, sagged, sank. After a moment or so she began to snore.

When she awoke it was dark. Silent, too, the only sound that of the occasional car passing beyond the shabby grass of the council block, the only light that coming in from the wire-protected bulb high on the ceiling of the walkway outside her window. Someone had drawn the curtains, but the light shone through.

For quite a long time Mrs. Davies could not work out what had happened. Why was she in her chair in the dark in the middle of the night? She must have dropped off. She began to pull herself out of the chair, and as she did so she remembered the two ladies from the Social Services. "My goodness!" she said.

"Whatever will they have thought! Dropping off like that! My goodness, what a muggins! Well, I never!"

She got to her feet, staggering a little because she had stiffened up over who-knew-how-long, and reached the light switch. The room sprang into non-committal presence, tidy and bright. "My goodness, look at the time! It's never eleven o'clock! My word, what a muggins! Whatever will they think!" She moved into the kitchen. "Cleared the tea things, washed up and all! Neat as a new pin. Fancy! That's ever so kind, that is. Well, I never, what a muggins!"

Then, as she shuffled about, slowly removing her layers of clothing and hauling herself into bed in due course with hot-water bottle and bedsocks, she remembered what the ladies had come for. The disability payments! From years back! Hundreds, the lady had said. Hundreds! An electric kettle? A winter coat with a nice fur collar? A television? No, she liked her wireless. A little holiday? Hundreds. Hundreds! Wouldn't Hubby have been pleased. Fancy!

Mrs. Davies fell asleep happy.

It was not until next day that she noticed the radio was missing. And the little milk jug, pink lustre with old-fashioned pictures on it, that had been on the tea tray and belonged to her great-gran. And the 1936 Coronation tea caddy and its matching mug. And over the next days, and even weeks, little by little, all the small things that had had any value: the brooch, the shoe buckles, the heavy old bangles and rings from the drawer in her bedroom, the musquash cape she'd worn at her wedding, the silver-backed clothes brush Aunt Nell had left her; her good shoes she never wore because they hurt her, the double oval silver frames holding photographs of her father and mother, stiff in high collar and huge flowered hat — but they had left her the photographs. And the little cache of her savings, safe she had thought hidden under the bread bin, ninety-two pounds, gone.

Mrs. Davies told no one. She had really no one to tell. Besides, she was too ashamed of having been so taken in. . . . And she was afraid people would think she was no longer fit to live on her own. . . .

2

Grace Bradby liked to get up early. "Up with the lark" she often said to Janice (but to no effect), although she had never heard a lark in her life, having always lived in cities. She was a woman of routine, the routines springing from a life of many ups and downs demanding adaptability and improvisation, and without routine she doubted she would have managed as well as she had. She was a tidy woman, in mind and in person. She liked to know what was what.

She put her feet out of bed and into the pink mules on the mat. The bed was large and sagged in the middle, but they had put the bolster down the centre of it which kept her and Janice almost as separate as they would have been in the single beds she would have preferred. But you can't have everything, and it was a nice big double room which had once had doors between its two halves, with a rudimentary kitchenette pressed into the front half of it behind a screen. Grace pulled on her dressing-gown and went to make some tea and a bit of toast.

The room was shabby, with dark greasy wallpaper and odd-lot furniture, but it was cheap because of some alarming cracks in the walls around the bay window, relics of a wartime bomb and the subsidence of badly built terrace houses. They were of yellowish London brick, six steps up to a porticoed front door, its panels furred with dust and never locked, built in the 1870s to meet the pretensions of ambitious senior clerks with large families. All were decaying, with short-time futures only as the local council procrastinated as to renovation or destruction; the one next door had been sealed up altogether with corrugated iron masking its windows and doors. Its garden was a mess of broken concrete, weeds and rubbish, but that on to which Grace looked out was not too bad, asphalted over behind a straggling privet hedge, black sacks of garbage usually inside their bins and a dejected-looking motorcycle up on its props, owned by the young man on the floor above who was seldom seen, like all the other lodgers. Grace made it her business to avoid them but that was not difficult, since some seemed to be out all the time while others seemed never to go out at all, only squeaking floorboards, and, from the top floor, bursts of rock music signalling human presence. Even the landlord was unknown, the rents being paid each Friday to an elderly Cypriot lady behind the counter of the newsagent's shop across the road, where the room had been advertised. There was also a launderette, a Pakistani hypermarket, a greengrocer, and the Underground only ten minutes' walk away. It was very convenient.

Grace sat in the window sunshine, smoking her after-breakfast cigarette and planning the day. It was being a nice spring, which made all the difference. Today was Tuesday. Tuesdays and Wednesdays she always went to work; they were her spying-out days. Thursdays and Fridays were action days, in and out, four to a day with luck. Then Saturday off-load it all, no hanging about, with the crowds and street markets and no one bothered too much about who and what.

She stubbed out her cigarette (she smoked only five a day, for she had seen what dependence can do when you're somewhere you can't get them), nipped down the passage to the toilet, returned and washed briskly at the sink behind the screen; dressed in a blouse and navy skirt, did her face modestly by the window in the back half of the room which overlooked a bigger garden, more neglected than the front, a jungle of grass and bushes which only cats used. She did not trouble too much about making a noise, for it was high time Janice stirred herself.

She rinsed out her cup and saucer, emptied the tea-leaves into the rubbish pail, took her navy coat from the hook behind the door, tied a scarf over her red-brown tinted hair and went and gave Janice a shake.

"It's gone half-past nine. Time you was up."

Janice groaned and turned away.

"Come along now, you lazy cow. I'm just off."

"What's the time?" She rolled on to her back and opened her eyes.

"Time you were up. It's your sign-on day too, don't forget, you don't want to get there so late you spend half the day queuing. And we need some shopping — sugar and a half of marge and we could do with some more instant."

"Okay." She sank back.

"Don't you lay back there, my girl. You get up and get moving, a nice sunny day like this. I think I'll go out Putney way today, it'll be nice by the river." She checked that she had her notebook and the *A* to *Z* guide in her handbag, snapped it shut and went to the door. "Best get a packet of Bronco too, while you're about it, right? Bye-bye."

She left the house and walked briskly to

Kentish Town Underground. One of the few good things about having turned sixty was the free travel pass, or the fares would have been crippling. At Embankment she changed on to the District line, waiting until the right train came along rather than be bothered by the intricacies of changing at Earl's Court. She was in nice time; no point in getting on site much before eleven, they didn't start coming out much before that, it took them so long to get moving. A nice day like this, she could take her time.

Although East Putney was the better area to work, she got out at Putney Bridge in order to look at the river. It glittered in the sunlight, and the blocks of flats and the trees along its edge seemed to glitter too, as did the buses trundling over the bridge and the flecks of mica in the pavements and the golden hands and figures on the twin church towers at either end, everything glittering and blowing in the strong April breeze. Days like this, work was a pleasure.

She crossed the bridge and walked up the High Street, looking in the shops and enjoying the differences between them and those in her own area. There were more dress shops, hairdressers, more continental delicacies behind high glass cases; it was a better class of place on the whole, but behind it lay still the small impoverished warrens of bed-sits and dingy flats, as yet ignored either by council planning or gentrification. It was just the right sort of area for her kind of work.

Briskly, she made for the public library.

It was warm in the main reading room, for the sun had been on the windows. Dust motes and, it seemed, breath hung in the old air. There was no sound save the rustle of pages turned and the wheezing of the four old people who sat at the central table with journals opened before them. Grace took a copy of *The Times* to an empty corner and sat down.

There were younger people in the room but Grace was not concerned with them. They were mostly there for a purpose, to study the appointments columns or the sports pages or even "Yesterday in Parliament." They seldom stayed long and barely disturbed the three elderly men and one woman at the table, who read each newspaper page slowly, one of the old men sunk down on himself asleep. The men were of no interest to Grace. Over "Letters to the Editor" she studied the woman.

Shabby. A turban-type hat that had once been powder-blue. A much neglected face. Gnarled hands with only a wedding ring deeply sunk below the knuckly joint. National Health specs.

No go.

The old man woke up and after awhile gathered himself together and shuffled out. So, presently, did the woman, revealing very old shoes — certainly no go. Grace read the arts page and an article about middle-class, middle-age childbirth. A Rastafarian and two teenage girls came briefly in and out. Another old woman came in and opened the *Daily Mail*.

Worn but tidy. A black felt hat and cheeks with rouge on them. A brooch on the lapel, only rubbish, but still . . . A wedding ring and a signet. A handbag that had once been good.

When the woman eventually left the library Grace followed her. She followed her into the High Street, into a supermarket (and bought a bar of chocolate), a chemist (small tablet of soap), into a side street, and another, past gardens, and to a large Victorian mansion bearing the sign: MARGARET POCOCK HOUSING TRUST.

No go.

Grace returned to the High Street, found a café and had a ham omelette, a Danish pastry and a cup of tea. Then just after two o'clock she walked till she found a betting shop and went in. They looked a rough lot mostly but with several women among them, studying the form sheets as she appeared to be doing. She did indeed place fifty pence each way on the 2:30 at Sandown, and leaned against the plastic and metal shelf littered with bits of paper, the stubs of pencils tethered with string, scorched tin ashtrays filled with butts, to wait till the result came in. The chatter of the loudspeaker relaying starting prices gave an air of hysteria to the shop but the atmosphere was of stoic calm, the clerks blasé behind their barriers, the clients all old hands.

An elderly woman stood near Grace, smoking with short puffs. Shapeless and shabby, she yet had an air of energy about her and her pouched eyes were bright. When the "Off" came and all noise died in the shop as the commentator's voice rose to its ritual scream, the woman gazed up at the television screen with fervour, her hands tight on the clasp of her handbag. The gabble increased, peaked, sank. Highland Prince had won.

The woman crushed out her cigarette on the floor, rushed to the pay clerk and thrust her betting-slip at him. Grace moved slightly nearer so that, in due course, she could see that the woman had backed the winner. She was shoving a nice wad of fivers into her handbag, her hands shaking, colour in her cheeks. She left the shop.

Grace, whose horse had not been in the first

three, followed. The woman hurried along the pavement and turned into a saloon bar. Grace waited at the bus stop just along the road until, after not long, the woman reappeared with two bottles protruding from her shopping bag and went off down a side street. She came to a terrace of small red brick villas, decent but run down, and turned into one with a broken gate between its privet. Grace walked past in time to see the front door close. The curtains at the various windows were all different and she could see five yellowed bits of card fixed above the single bell-push.

She walked on to the corner of the road, then stopped, took out the notebook from her handbag and made a note of the address. Then she had a look in the *A* to *Z*, found her way back to the High Street. It was still a lovely day although not a very useful one: she'd been on her feet a long time and nothing much to show for it. She decided to pack it in, took a 14 bus to Warren Street and the Underground from there home. Janice was out, so Grace made herself a cup of tea and listened to "PM" on the radio.

3

Grace and Janice had met in Holloway Prison. Grace was doing six months for larceny, Janice three for the most recent of a series of clumsy shop-liftings.

Grace was released first and found a rather nasty room in King's Cross where, a week later, Janice joined her. Something about Janice appealed to Grace, who was some thirty years older; she was so utterly clueless. "You've no more sense than a new-born baby," she declared when Janice brought home a blouse and two pairs of tights from Oxford Street only ten days after she'd been released. "There's no need to do that sort of thing while you're with me. You remember that now, and don't never do it again. I mean it."

Grace needed someone like Janice to work this scheme she'd devised during the last weeks in prison, fruit of the various periods of legitimate employment she'd had over the years since the war. The longest job had been over two years at an old people's home from which she had been dismissed at last when the new matron proved sharper than Grace had thought. No charges brought, too embarrassing for the home, privately funded and run. Other jobs of the same kind had followed (she gave herself excellent references) but last year, after a longish run as a home help, the wretched DHSS had landed her in Holloway. The DHSS was very strict on home helps, and although no one could deny she was first-rate at her work — neat and quick and kindly, a favourite with the old folk — nevertheless she got six months, the clock and transistor and other things being found still in her room. Never one to crumble under adversity, she had used the time to do some constructive thinking.

Grace had been born, the eldest of five, in one of a terrace of ugly villas on the outskirts of Chelmsford. Her father worked for the railway and in his spare time cultivated a too-large plot of heavy soil from which he wrenched mud-stained, slug-nibbled vegetables of the less palatable kind. His children were made to help him in this, lugging water cans and wheelbarrows full of earth-knotted weeds, struggling to dig the great sodden clods of earth with tools too big for them, their feet clammy inside the Wellingtons that had always belonged to someone else first — in the case of Grace, her father. Her mother never came out into the allotment but stayed inside the house, smoking cigarettes and reading the women's magazines passed on to her by a neighbour who cleaned a doctor's surgery — the pages hardly held together by the time Grace's mother got them. Few serials ever began or finished, and recipes for Christmas dinner turned up during August. Mostly, one of the children, usually Grace, was sent to do the household shopping; and most evenings father and mother went to the nearby pub, Mum on her own if Dad were on night shift.

When Grace was fourteen Mum's parents came to live with them. Grandma had had a stroke, Grand-dad could not cope. The front parlour was made into their bedroom and was soon suffused with their particular odour of wintergreen, tobacco and unwashed flesh. Grandma had another stroke and died of it; Grand-dad remained. He was a disgusting old man and had been a disgusting young one, cunning, a bully, envious of all who had done better than he. As the eldest, it was Grace who had to do most for him and learned to deal dispassionately with horny toenails, unwashed dentures and the whining lechery that remained in him from his youth.

As soon as she left school she got a job, at

first in a bakery, then behind the marble counters of the butter and cheese department of a nationwide chain of provision merchants. The cool bare hygiene of it all, the crisp slap and pat of the wooden spatulas moulding the butter into bricks, the hiss and clunk of the wooden-handled wire cutting through cheese just suited her. Trim in her overall, her hair tied up in butter muslin, she was like a nurse in an operating theatre, efficient and nicely spoken — she had early realised that BBC English was desirable. As soon as she felt her job was secure she left home and went into lodgings — a small dark room with only a gas ring, but no more mud, Wellingtons, siblings and Grand-dad. She never went home again, not even at Christmas.

She made a few friends among the staff; there was the cinema and the dance hall, and she took evening classes in bookkeeping, for she had her eye on a cashier's job before too long. But then came the war.

At first it made little difference. She was not one to get excited over anything and went on in the way that suited her while giving thought to the fact that, with men going off to the forces, her prospects of a better job were enhanced. The town, the whole of East Anglia, began to fill up with servicemen, bringing a new flavour to the street and dance

33

halls. Some girls got very silly; Grace did not, picking and choosing her escorts and allowing absolutely no liberties — let any man mess her about like Grand-dad had tried, no thank you!

Then one day she suddenly got fed up — fed up with the blackout and the randy servicemen and the customers moaning about rationing and the elderly woman cashier whose job she wanted but knew she'd never get now the men were being conscripted and the woman was well dug in. It was the old ones who were getting the jobs now, the young ones being whisked off into the forces. So she went out and volunteered for the NAAFI and spent the next four years in canteens and billets up and down the country, part of the huge, clanging, steaming machine that, before she was in it, she had thought would have something in common with butter and cheese.

Well, so it had in a way. It was certainly better than square-bashing in a baggy uniform and keeping your hair rolled up off the back of your collar, better than being bawled at by bossy cows who tried to be officers and ending up maybe on a gun site somewhere where it never stopped raining. It taught her to distance herself even more from her fellows, to despise their silliness, and prize her own dispassion higher than ever. She learned a lot; it wasn't all bad. The only bad thing was Harold, and he didn't last long; he had been an army cook and they had married soon after they were both demobbed. She must have been mad.

Well, that was all water under the bridge. She had made a living one way or another over the years, mainly by always looking out for Number One. There had been some close shaves sometimes but she had always kept her head; she had quite enjoyed the periods of regular employment that had entitled her to the pension and the travel pass and supplementary too, should she ever decide to claim it — which she never would, for she was wary of signing official forms of any kind. Once they had your name on a form . . . Which was how this present scheme had come to her, keeping herself to herself in Holloway after that cow of a DHSS supervisor had landed her there, and bored out of her mind. She had thought the scheme up, and realised she would need a partner, for two women ringing your doorbell are more reassuring than one. But it would be her scheme and she would be boss, and Janice, clueless and vague, was just right.

It was a good scheme, watertight and surprisingly profitable. Grace had worked out the places where suitable subjects might be found; as well as betting shops and libraries there were bingo halls and supermarkets, jumble sales, the post office on pension days and, in fine weather, park benches. Her eye was trained and she was seldom wrong in assessing the probable worth of those she marked down. It was amazing what the old dears had salted away that they didn't know the value of, small things mostly but they all mounted up. And there was nearly always cash concealed in places Grace well knew how to find, an amazing sum sometimes — she had once got 827 pounds from under a mattress a dog wouldn't sleep on. The tricky part was where they lived; almshouses and homes were no good, even council flats could be dicey if neighbours or children were about. The bed-sitter in a terraced house split up into lodgings was ideal, and on the whole Grace was usually lucky. She had an instinct for such things.

Once the front door opened the rest was easy; she could have done it with her eyes shut now, after nearly three months' experience. A passport photo stuck on a piece of card with plenty of lettering on it (never mind what, the old things never examined it, although in fact it did read like something official, for Grace liked to do things properly), a briefcase full of papers covered with figures, her own authority and pleasant manner, and they were almost always admitted. Then it was simply a question of marking time, dazzling the old things with jargon and the prospect of good fortune; they supplied their own details, along which Grace advanced as delicately as a spider spinning its thread. The old dears were happy, talking away and full of joy at what she told them; and meanwhile Janice went quietly about her business, spying out the trinkets, the transistors and pretty ornaments, then bringing in the tea tray with the powdered sleeping pills already in the cup. It never took much more than fifteen or twenty minutes for the old dears to fall asleep, and after that they were home and dry. There were always plenty of plastic carrier bags around to carry the things away in, apart from their own hold-alls. No one ever took any notice of women with hold-alls.

Sometimes it failed, of course. Sometimes you got a really nasty suspicious type who wouldn't let you in because she didn't know you. Well, win some, lose some. Sometimes they had nothing really worth bothering with so you left them having a nice sleep and none the worse for it, although a bit disappointed probably as the days passed and the promised windfall didn't come. Men were right out. She'd tried men once or twice when she first started the scheme, but they were a dead loss. They seldom had anything of any value, their rooms were often either bare or disgusting and one old horror had tried to put his hand up her skirt as she poured the tea. They could turn nasty too; even an old man could be surprisingly strong. No, men were out.

It was a livelihood which comprised skill, nerve, an understanding and manipulation of human nature and risk. The risk made Grace Bradby's cold blood run warmer and faster; deep out of sight behind her calm façade, the stalking, the hunt, the kill thrilled her. It was absolute power dependent on absolute skill. Besides, if all went well, it was roughly five thousand a year tax free.

The trickiest part was disposal, but there Grace had many years of experience and had built up a number of contacts. There were the small, dusty jewellers' shops tucked into crannies of the older congeries of London, some of them regular fences, some pretending not; the pawnshops if necessary, although they were not really good business; and, of course, the street markets. There, amid the streaming kaleidoscope of people, objects of every kind could be bought and sold with total indifference. A name was seldom asked for, and if it was it was never the true one. Objects sank and rose on the tide of goods heaped up on

the stalls; everything had a market with someone, from a coneyskin cape to a pinchbeck
brooch. Like their wares, some of the stall-
holders came and went too, faceless young
people flogging World War II impedimenta
or oriental skirts or homemade pottery, or
quick-talking youths with cartons of T-shirts,
folding umbrellas or tapes, transient as the
lorries their goods fell off. But many were permanent, tough professionals who made a decent living out of it. Some of these Grace
had got to know over the years. They asked
no questions, she told them no lies; they gave
her a fair price, for she never offered them
anything for which there was not, sooner or
later, a buyer.

From time to time the police came through
the markets on the lookout for stolen property;
but the kinds of things Grace dealt in were
too insignificant to catch their eyes, and in
any case had probably never even been reported as stolen.

That, really, was the beauty of Grace's
scheme. Like as not, the old dears didn't
even know they'd been robbed for quite
a time after her visit, and then they probably
thought they'd mislaid whatever it was, forgotten where they'd put it. And even when
(and if) they did realise what had been
done, they were too confused and ashamed

to tell anyone. For if an old lady comes into a police station, agitated and probably deaf, and says she can't find her hubby's watch and chain that she's sure she always kept in a shoe box at the back of the wardrobe but hadn't actually set eyes on since she couldn't remember when, what sort of a tale is that? Two ladies called from the Social Services about her disability, or was it her fuel allowance or her orthopaedic aids, and she'd never heard any more from them, and her regular socal worker knew nothing about it. She'd never seen them before or since and she was sure she'd had hubby's watch in that shoebox; and her pension money had gone too. But might she not have spent it? She might, but she thought not, it was only the Thursday. But she couldn't be sure? Well, it was some days ago now, a week or so maybe before she noticed, the watch, that is, the money she kept hidden away till Fridays when she went shopping. The police were usually kind and patient and fatherly to the old lady twice their age; and made a note of it all which vanished into the interstices of the system; and privately thought there was probably something in it that would bear keeping track of, but not much to be done. The old lady went away. She couldn't be sure it wasn't her fault somehow. The incident remained on record and that was that.

It was a nice way of making a living.

Janice went along with it. She went along with whatever happened to her, always had, a jellyfish in a tepid sea. She had grown up in Nottingham where her mother, a lumpish sort of woman, was rather glad when her husband eventually deserted her, for the only way she could think of for not having a baby or a miscarriage every year was to be without him. Janice had six brothers and sisters, of which she was the middle girl, and from the age of ten until she ran away from home at fifteen she had been interfered with by her uncle, her mother's brother Charley, who, when the husband ran off, more or less took charge of the family. Janice quite liked Uncle Charley and passively accepted what he liked to do to her. It was only some weeks after she'd left home, in a layby off the motorway, paying in kind for a lift Londonwards in a van belonging to a central heating firm, that she realized there was much more to it than Uncle Charley had ever ventured. The whole thing left her cold; and as she spent the next few years largely in and out of the care of various authorities, she never had much occasion to change her view. She whored when she had to but in an amateurish way; mostly she drifted in and out of unskilled jobs, with shoplifting and petty thieving to help out, living in squats or lodging-houses. She was arrested several times, of course, but put on probation; until the last time, which proved too much for everyone, and she found herself in Holloway, twenty-six, of no fixed address, family long lost sight of, a dreamy girl of no particular looks or preferences, not, on the whole, disliking prison, which at least saved her the effort of having to make decisions about anything. But some of the women frightened her. Working alongside Grace Bradby in the laundry, she was grateful for her protection; and joining her in the room she found for them afterwards saved a lot of bother. She felt safe with Grace. Grace was what a mother ought to be, authoritative, capable and kind. And sexless. The bolster down the middle of the double bed could have been of concrete.

She had never known any old people. Grandparents were dead or gone when she was a child and Uncle Charley had been only middle-aged. When Grace had outlined her scheme to her, Janice had asked, "But won't they catch on?"

"Not them! You wouldn't believe the number of people those old dears have to see. They don't know who half of them are most of the time, and they're only too glad to have someone to talk to anyway. Don't you worry, Jan. I know what I'm doing."

"Yes, well, but . . . I mean, they'll have seen us and all. What if they call the cops?"

"They're not going to do that while we're there, are they, because it's not till long after we're gone they'll even begin to think there's something funny. All they'll think at first is they've had a nice long sleep. A lot of the things they won't even notice have gone till days afterwards, if then. And even if they do and go trotting off to report it, no one pays much attention to old folks nowadays. It's not as if it's the crown jewels they're losing."

Janice yielded, as she always did. Grace had such confidence, and with all her experience in the homes and that she must know what she was about.

"You'll see, Jan. It'll go like a dream. Just keep your mouth shut and leave it to me."

And indeed it had gone like a dream for several months now. Grace's planning, her preliminary groundwork, her judgement of suitable subjects and, not least of all, the actual performance, her neat and kindly aspect, had carried them through with hardly ever a hitch. They never worked in their own area, they never worked more than a couple of weeks in the same district, but spied, moved in, cleaned up, moved on. By the time any complaints might have come in they were long gone.

Of course there were occasional setbacks. They stood on the terracotta-tiled path of an Edwardian terrace house to which Grace had followed a subject two days before and rang the bottom bell — you could reckon an old person didn't live on an upper floor. It was marked Andrews in faded ink, and when presently the front door opened Grace put on her smile and asked: "Miss Andrews?"

"Yes."

"We're from the Social Services."

"Yes?"

"I wonder if we might come in for a moment?"

"Why?"

Miss Andrews was squat, with a square leathery face and a crop of white hair cut like a man's. Grace instantly realised that, although she was lame and had walked with a stick all the way when Grace had trailed her from the post office, she was not frail.

She lowered her voice. "It's about your disability."

"Disability?"

"Your . . ." She gestured discreetly towards the stick.

"That's not a disability. That's arthritis. I'm

not disabled." She made as if to close the door.

Grace said quickly, "Not within the meaning of the Disabled Persons Act, but you're entitled to benefits."

The door paused. "Benefits?"

"Yes. Might we come in? It's not very private standing here on the doorstep."

"Very well." Miss Andrews turned her back and stumped away down the passage to the back room. It was a bed-sitter, neat and spartan as a ship's cabin, a screen in one corner hiding a gas ring and basin. There was a pair of good brass candlesticks on the mantelpiece, where a gas fire wheezed, a good radio on a stool beside the bed. "Who did you say you were?"

"I'm Mrs. Black from the DHSS and this is my colleague Mary. We're from group OAP B22, which I don't think you'll have heard of before, it's newly set up, you see, to see what can be done to help those falling outside the usual services."

"Where's your identification?" said Miss Andrews, leaning on her stick.

"Right here, dear." Grace took the card out of her handbag and passed it over. Janice nervously moved back towards the door as Miss Andrews studied the card, but Grace remained composed.

"Flimsy thing. Looks like a phoney."

Grace smiled, holding out her hand to receive it back. "I'm afraid it does. It's all this cutting down on government spending, you see, the department tries to make do with its own documentation and not have the expense of all that HMS printing and leaflets and special cards and so on. It all helps Mr. Lawson to balance his budget, I suppose, but it does put us social workers in a bit of an embarrassing situation sometimes, as you can see. We just have to grin and bear it and rely on people's good sense. May we sit down?"

"I suppose so."

They sat. Grace opened her briefcase, spread out her documents and began her spiel.

When she got to the words "disability allowance" Miss Andrews interrupted. "I'm not disabled."

"Well no, of course not. Like I said, not within the meaning of the original act you're not, but there's this new order, you see, a subsection of the National Health Act of 1981 just brought into force — well, not just, of course, because it was brought in 1981 but the DHSS is only just beginning to get round to applying it to all borderline cases like yourself, you see, we're so short-staffed now with the government cutbacks I'm afraid it's taking far too long for us to get round to everyone with entitlement."

"I don't need charity," said Miss Andrews. She opened a packet of cigarettes and lit up, waving the match out aggressively.

"It's not charity, dear, it's entitlement. It's an allowance paid to all those over retirement age as a legal entitlement. But if so wished the allowance can be waived and the benefits be received in kind rather than cash."

"What kind?"

"What kind of kind, eh? I can see you've got a sense of humour, Miss Andrews, can't you, Mary? I often think that of all God's gifts a sense of humour's the most precious. Well now . . ." She shuffled her papers around. "What kind of kind?" She gave a little chuckle. "What kind of kind depends on the degree of entitlement and, of course, on the special requirements of the benefitee. Now in your case . . ." She broke off. "Miss Andrews, I wonder if you'd be ever so kind and let Mary here make us all a cup of tea? We've been on our feet since I don't know when today and we've still another call to make, and a cup of tea would be a wonder. Mary . . ."

Janice got to her feet to move towards the screen but Miss Andrews said loudly, "No you don't!"

"Pardon?"

"She's not going in my kitchen."

"Just to put the kettle on, dear."

"Not in my kitchen."

"Perhaps you'd like to do it yourself then, although we're only trying to save you trouble."

"My pleasure," said Janice faintly.

"I'm not having anyone messing about in my kitchen," said Miss Andrews loudly. "Besides, if you ask me it's all a load of codswallop. All this benefitees and entitlement and Department of This and by-laws of That. Codswallop!"

"It's the law of the land, dear."

"Codswallop! There's nothing I need that I can't get for myself That's what's wrong with this country. Everyone's got their hand out waiting for the state to put something in it. Lot of grafters and spongers. I was brought up to work hard, earn a good wage and put it by for my old age and that's what I've done. I don't need government charity, handing out this and that. I've got my pension and by golly I earned it, and now it comes back to me with a bit of what I put by myself and that's all I need, thank you very much. If the government cut down on all this namby-pamby charity handouts and made people responsible for their own lives this country'd be a better place to live in like it was during the war, and all you lot would be out doing a proper job."

Grace, lips narrowed, gathered her papers together and put them back in her briefcase. "Well, if you feel like that, dear . . ."

"Don't call me dear. I'm not your dear. My name's Elizabeth Andrews and I'll wish you good day."

"I'm sorry you take it this way, Miss Andrews," Grace said. With dignity she rose, upped up the briefcase and moved to the door, which Janice had already opened. "I'm afraid you're doing yourself out of your rights in this matter. It's every citizen's privilege to receive what the state says he's entitled to, but if that's the way you feel about it, then I shall say no more. Come, Mary. Goodbye, Miss Andrews. I'm sorry you won't let us help."

They shut the door behind them, went down the passage past the stairs and the hall stand hung with dusty coats, the closed door of the front room, a carton of empty soft drink bottles, and let themselves out into the street.

"What an old cow," said Grace as they walked briskly away.

"I didn't like it when she looked at your card," said Janice.

"Silly old faggot! They can't see anything, most of them, without their specs on. Still, we'd best not hang about, she could turn nasty."

They turned into the main road towards the Underground; Grace never liked to stay on in an area where a job had not worked out.

They did not speak much on the journey back across London and the walk back home. There was afternoon calm in the streets, and their room, with its shabby, unmatched furniture, was sunny and safe. Janice went down the passage to the toilet while Grace lit a cigarette and put the kettle on — a nice electric one they'd acquired a month or so ago.

When Janice returned Grace said, "And we never even got a cup of tea."

"I got this, though." From the pocket of her jeans Janice brought out a locket, chased gold with a daisy of seed pearls round a tiny turquoise heart. One of the pearls was missing.

"You what?"

"I got this."

"You silly bitch!" She came swiftly and snatched the locket from Janice's hand, studying it. "What'd you want to do that for, with her acting up and all?"

"It was just laying there, on the chest by the door, all mixed up with hair-grips and pills and rubbish. She'll never miss it."

"How do you know? She's just the kind of old girl who would miss it, belonged to her mother or something. Honest, Jan, you ought to have more sense."

Janice looked sullen. "It's got no chain on nor nothing, she never wore it. It was just laying there."

"You listen to me, my girl. I've told you before and I'll tell you again. When a job starts to go wrong we leave it, right? No messing about, no trying to make something out of it after all, just cut our losses and out. O-U-T out, and fast. Right?"

"Yes, but . . ."

"No buts. Out. I've got more sense in my little finger than you have in your whole head, and when I tell you to do something you bloody do it or else you're out on your own, right?"

"I thought . . ."

"Don't. Leave the thinking to me and we'll both be okay. You don't know your arse from your elbow, left on your own. You've no more sense than a newborn kitten."

Tears began to fill Janice's eyes.

Grace held the locket out to her. "Here, take it. I don't want nothing to do with it. You nicked it, you get rid of it, it's not going in with any of my stuff." Janice took the trinket and put it back in her pocket. "You get rid of it up the market somewhere tomorrow. I don't want it laying around here and I won't handle it, not after her acting up like that. You ought to have more sense."

"It was just laying there."

"Oh for God's sake, girl, make the tea and belt up!" Grace went into the back room and took off her shoes. "Tomorrow, right? While I'm selling off, you go somewhere else and get rid of it quick, right?"

Janice silently made the tea, which they drank without further speech, then went sulkily into the bedroom, lay down and soon fell asleep; she had a talent for sleep. Grace sat on in the window, through whose dirty panes the sun fell pleasantly, smoking, watching the street. Like a child, Janice was sometimes. No more sense . . . Still, no harm done probably. Like Jan said, the old cow would likely never miss it, with nothing else gone. A wasted afternoon, although the morning had gone all right — two visits and some useful bits and pieces and quite a nice sum in cash. And the day before had been satisfactory too, each call rewarding. A good week, on balance. . . .

The weekend markets were always good. Plenty of people, plenty of business, the crowds too thick and sluggish for any member of it to be remembered, the noise too raucous for any bargaining to be overheard. Transactions were always quick; neither the buyer nor

Grace wished to hang about, those who knew what they were doing least of all. And Grace knew her market — which dealers liked transistors, which silver, which Victoriana or old-fashioned fur pieces. Grace would often note that the articles she had disposed of when she started up the street had already been sold by the time she passed the stall on her way back. Jewellery and smaller objects she kept for the little shops with windows full of dusty clocks and watches, frail wire grilles on their doors, dusky within save for the one strong lamp on the bench behind the counter, strewn with the intestines of clocks of all kinds.

To these she went alone, but Janice came with her to the markets, loitering along the stalls, occasionally nicking things, while Grace did the business. But this she did not let Grace know, not since the first time when Grace had let fly at her, slapped her across the face. Grace had very strong views about fouling your own doorstep.

But with Miss Andrews' little pendant Grace sent her off on her own, forbidding her the market. "I'm not taking the risk, Jan. You nicked it, you get rid of it."

"You're bonkers," Janice had said sullenly, twisting a lock of hair round and round her finger as she always did when she was nervous. "You're paranoiac."

53

"That's right. That's just what I am. And that's why you and me's been doing all right, right?" She had sat on the arm of a chair and regarded Janice indulgently, for her anger had cooled and she knew very well that Jan was completely her creature. The knowledge warmed her into something quite like affection, such as she might have felt for a cat or a budgerigar. "You're a silly juggins, Jan. You want to go back in the nick, is that it, with all them screws and dykes and broken-down old tarts? That what you want? If it is, then you're on your own, girl. You can kiss me goodbye." Janice twisted her hair in silence. "So off you go now and get rid of that bit of rubbish — and do go a good long way off too. I don't want it anywhere near our own doorstep, right? Right."

But Janice did not go far, only a couple of bus stops. She was cross with Grace for speaking to her like that. She was often cross with Grace, who seemed to think Janice was some kind of moron or something. Of course it was great to have Grace running things; Janice had always found the effort of running her life too much for her, which was why she had ended up in Holloway. Grace was sharp as a needle and took care of everything. But while pleased to surrender to Grace's authority, Janice enjoyed resenting it. Who did she think she was?

Both Grace and Janice knew very well who she was; she was the boss, the brains of their agreeable life-style. But she ought not to speak to Janice like that, like she was some kind of moron or something.

So Janice went sulkily off to a small street market only a mile or two from where they lived. They sometimes shopped there; it was mostly fruit and vegetables, with cheap clothing stalls as well, and a stall of the usual junk run by a fat young man with sharp eyes. He watched her as she loitered.

"Anything you fancy, love?"

"Might be."

"Some nice bangles?"

"Not my style. I'm selling really."

He cooled. "Like what?"

She brought out the locket and unwrapped its screw of paper. "It was my gran's."

He looked at it coldly, not touching it where it lay in her open hand. "Not interested, love."

"It's gold."

"I can see that. It'd get nicked off here inside five minutes. Sorry."

She wrapped it up, shrugging. "Okay," she said, and drifted off. Stuff it! Stuff Grace. Still . . .

A narrow doorway, a dusty window showing alarm clocks and modest rings. She went in.

From a cubbyhole an elderly man emerged.

"D'you buy things?"

"That depends, darling. What you got?"

She unwrapped it. He took it in his gnarled paw, holding it close to his eyes. "There's a stone missing."

"It was my gran's."

"Still a stone missing. Easy to spot. Not interested, darling."

"It's antique."

"I don't doubt. So am I. But I got no stones missing." He smiled a wonderfully virile smile and put the locket back in her hand with both his, drawing her slightly towards him over the counter. "You come back after closing time, I show you. No stones missing."

She pulled away. "Do you mind!"

"You come back, maybe I buy."

She gave him a scornful look and left the shop, slamming the door behind her in the hope the glass might crack. Dirty pig!

That was it, then. She really didn't feel like bothering any more. Grace could stuff it. Grace need not know. Stuff Grace.

Around eight o'clock that evening she sat on a bar stool in the King's Crown saloon bar, a vodka and Coke half drunk before her. Muzak and the hum of voices, the warm heavy air and the dim lighting made an agreeable buffer between her and the rest of the world, through which she was nevertheless aware of a creeping depression. No one had spoken to her, no one had done more than give her a glance; she was not going anywhere or meeting anyone, for this was not her usual patch, too far from home to be local but too near to be entirely strange, which was why she had come here — on the chance of drifting into a familiar group and also to spite Grace. Grace would be wild if she knew Janice had tried to offload anything so near home, she would never do business on what she called her own doorstep. Grace would be wild too if she knew the pendant was still in the pocket of Janice's jeans. Janice certainly didn't feel like going back home and spending the rest of the evening watching telly with Grace. Grace had really upset her, tearing a strip off her like that. Stuff Grace.

She bought a packet of crisps and looked around for likely company. The pub was only half full, groups noisy together and couples who plainly did not want outsiders. But there was a man alone now at a table from which some people had just left, so Janice took her drink and the crisps, slid from the stool and wandered over.

"This free?"

The man nodded but did not speak, leaning back against the wall with his head bent, watching his fingers turn and turn again the half empty glass of lager on the table before him.

She sat down on the chair still warm from the previous occupant, took a sip of her drink and studied him obliquely. He was quite a dish, thirtyish, shortish dark hair, properly shaved, collar and tie with a boring tweed jacket and tan slacks. He took no notice of her, didn't even shift his feet stretched out under the table, but remained withdrawn in his thoughts.

She took some crisps, then held the packet out to him. "Like some?"

"What? Oh-ta." He reached forward and took one. They munched together in silence. Then he seemed to feel he should say something. "Nice evening."

"Yes."

Each took a sip of their drinks; Janice's was nearly gone and she could fancy another, but he was unaware. He was going to be a dead loss, just not interested, and she felt depression come up in a wave again. She was suddenly desperate.

"You look proper browned off."

"Sorry?"

"I said you look proper browned off. Like

someone died or something."

"Well, you have a point. They almost did."

Her turn now. "Sorry?"

"Almost died. Mate of mine. I've just been at the hospital, visiting."

"Oh, sorry. Bad, is he?"

"Not too bad now. Broken arm, concussion. They thought he had internal injuries but that's okay now."

"In an accident, was he?"

"Yeah. Got dragged. Nasty."

"What a shame."

"Yeah."

They both drank.

"Work together, do you?" she said at last.

"Yeah."

"What work d'you do, then?"

"Well — Civil Service, kind of."

"Civil, are you?" She giggled, a bit desperately.

"Yeah. Ever so civil." He looked at her for the first time, making an effort to be cheerful. "Drink up and I'll get you another."

She drank up quickly, then watched him go to the bar and successfully catch the barman's attention, something not a lot of men were good at. He wasn't tall but he had nice shoulders. His hair was nice. It was nice him being upset about his mate.

He returned with the drinks.

"What sort of work d'you do, then?"

"Well — let's say I'm in communications."

"What, Telecom and that?"

"Something like. What about you? Model, show girl, telly person?"

"You're having me on."

"No, honest." But he was.

She drank, not best pleased. "Actually I have done some modelling." She had often thought her legs were just as good as those she saw, seven feet high, on the platform walls of the Underground. "For magazines and that."

"Yeah?"

"Yeah."

His attention drifted away, his mind perhaps still on his sick friend. He had nice eyes, not sufficiently fixed on her. If he was dressed more casual he'd be smashing. She tried again. "I'm a secretary really. Well, personal assistant. In films." She had gone into an employment bureau once on impulse, having seen such a job written up on a board outside — eight thousand a year it paid. But they hadn't even taken her name. "It's ever so interesting. I meet all the stars."

"No kidding."

She had the feeling he didn't believe her. She finished her drink. "I'm on sick leave now.

With my back. I've got a long back, see, and it keeps going out."

"Where's it go to?"

"Sorry?"

"Sorry — just a joke."

"Oh — yeah." The pub had filled up and everyone seemed to be having a good time, ready for a great night. She was hungry and would like a scampi-in-a-basket or maybe a Chinese and then go on to a disco somewhere — he looked as if he could afford it. And then if he wanted to she'd quite fancy it, he had nice clean fingernails . . .

He looked at his watch, a digital. "Sorry, love, I must love you and leave you." He pushed back his chair and stood up. "I'm on duty at eight — unsocial hours, flexible rostering, whatever." He grinned down at her, for her dismay was childishly apparent. "See ya around maybe."

"Yeah, maybe." It was as though she'd stepped on a stair that wasn't there. "Tomorrow maybe?"

"Could be, while my mate's still in hospital."

"Yeah."

"Well, seeya." He swung away through the crowd, moving confidently between the jostling drinkers. Janice watched him go with astonishing regret. Not only was her evening now up the spout but she had really fancied him.

Next evening she was back at the King's Crown. It held a Sunday night crowd, quiet and hard-drinking, fortifying themselves for the week to come. She wore her best jeans and a lurex-threaded pullover and great big earrings dangling under her long hair, which she had tried to puff up a bit to look like Julia Somerville on the nine o'clock news. She got there a bit before she reckoned hospital visiting hours ended, and took her drink to a padded bench in a corner, watching the door. A couple of men tried to pick her up but she froze them off.

He did not come.

The bar grew fuller. She began to feel conspicuous, spinning out her drink, avoiding the eyes and the innuendoes and the people who wanted her seat.

And then he did.

She was so pleased that she stood up, waving, and shouted "Hi!"

He grinned and raised his hand, then went direct to the bar and brought the glasses over to where she now sat, triumphant as a child.

"Hi there." He squeezed in beside her. He was dressed more casually this evening, a sweater and jeans. She thought he looked great. "So, how's things?"

"Okay. How's your friend?"

"Better. He'll be okay."

"Is he married?"

"No. Why?"

"It'd be tough on his wife if he's badly injured and that."

"Yeah. Yeah, it would."

Around them in the smoky light everyone was having a good time, but he let the pause lengthen and she could think of nothing to say. Despite her hopes, she hadn't really expected him to turn up; her experience was that men seldom did what they said they would, especially if it was pleasant. She was used to disappointment, accepted it as natural. But here he was — and she could think of nothing to hold him.

At last he said, "So what's new?"

"Not a lot. Have you had a nice day?"

"Been working."

"What, on a Sunday?"

"I told you, unsocial hours. What about you, nine to five?"

"I told you, I'm on sick leave with my back. As a matter of fact, I'm thinking of packing it in."

"What, that glitzy job?"

"It's not all that great really. They take advantage."

"Well, they would, wouldn't they." They

drank in silence again.

She asked, "D'you live around here?"

"No. I only dropped in 'cause it's near the hospital. You?"

"Not really. More Camden Town way." Grace had always drummed into her to keep basic information like that vague. "I live with my auntie. I'm an orphan."

"Tough."

"I don't remember them really, I was only a kid. In a car crash, it was."

"There's more people killed on the roads than die of lung cancer."

"D'you smoke?"

"No. I want to keep my health and beauty."

"You look ever so fit. D'you jog?"

"Sometimes."

"There's jogging all over. You can't go anywhere these days without some sweaty great man jogging past you."

"They don't turn you on?"

"Not when they're all wet and sweaty in what look like underpants they don't."

"I wear an elegant track suit. All my sweating's done inside."

"Thanks very much, I can live without it!"

The exchange had warmed them up a bit, and he looked at her with more interest. "What say we go and have a curry somewhere? Unless your auntie's got something on the hob?"

Her pale skin flushed. "Great. You're not working?"

"Not tonight. I'm on day shifts this week. Bar crises, that is. Shall we move?"

"Okay." She slid along the bench over the warm bit where he had been sitting; it felt lovely.

He drove an ugly blue Volkswagen, rather a disappointment to her; she had expected something more flashy. They ate in a murky Indian restaurant where the waiters knew him and shone their teeth at him. He told her the food was very good and with enthusiasm ate a huge selection of platefuls, most of them too hot for her; she was glad of an ice cream. She spun him some tales about herself which seemed to amuse him; she had the feeling that he was laughing at her but not in a nasty way, simply as though he didn't believe half of what she was telling him — in which, of course, he was right. She trailed a question or two about himself, but apart from the fact that his name was Dave and he was on shift work, learned little. She didn't press it, partly because she knew men never liked being asked personal questions and anyway seldom told the truth, but mainly because she wanted to hold him.

He was lovely. He was clean and tidy and he didn't seem really interested in her, only with half his mind almost and as though he felt it would be rude to ditch her. She was not used to this kind of treatment; men either picked you up and got on with it or they didn't pick you up at all. Dave was different, intriguing. He had a lovely smile.

"You've got a lovely smile," she said, then flushed, feeling a fool.

But he only laughed, paying the bill. "Come on," he said, "I'll run you home."

Remembering Grace's strictures about never telling anyone anything about themselves but not wanting to walk, she told him Kentish Town. She had hoped he might suggest a disco or something first, but was quite content to let him get straight to the sex. He drove, however, to Kentish Town Underground, slowed and asked, "Where now?"

She didn't know what to say. "This'll do."

"Don't be daft, where d'you live?"

"Just round the corner."

He drove round the corner. "You don't live here, love." It was all closed shops and a secondhand-car park.

"This'll do. Honest."

He drew into the kerb. "What's the matter, afraid to be seen with me?" He was still amused.

"It's not that. It's just my auntie — she's, well, you know . . ."

"Okay, okay." He leaned across and opened the passenger door. No groping, no heaving, no messing about . . . There was nothing for her to do but get out. He grinned up at her through the window.

"See ya."

"I go there most nights."

"Okay."

"If you're visiting your friend . . ."

"Could be."

"Well — thanks for the food."

"No sweat. Mind how you go."

She could do nothing but slam the door and walk away up the street. He revved the engine and drove past her, tooting the horn as he went. She waved. What a let down! It wasn't hardly eleven o'clock! She ought to feel insulted but she didn't. He was a mystery, acting like that, a mystery man. He was really nice. She really fancied him.

It was two or three weeks before Grace noticed that Janice was not quite as she had been. Although they lived so closely together, they were not friends. Their self-absorption was so intense that neither of them had the least curiosity about anyone else; their association was a day-to-day affair, a practical arrangement in which Grace was mistress, Janice maid. What Janice did in her own time was of no concern to Grace, provided it did not endanger Grace's scheme. If Janice sometimes came home very late, or even not until the morning, muzzy, smelling of drink and men, Grace merely tightened her lips and said nothing. She had never cared for sex herself but recognised it as the only coinage at times for soppy girls like Janice.

But lately Janice had been different, moony yet edgy, tarting herself up some evenings and rushing off all starry-eyed only to return glumly long before closing time.

"You're early," Grace would say. "Quiet, was it?"

"Yeah. No one showed," and she would take herself off to bed. Janice could opt out in sleep any time.

Even, it seemed, on her feet. Grace had to speak to her sharply. "You need to keep your eyes on the ball, girl," she said as they came away from what had been a rewarding block of council flats one working day. "You nearly messed that one up."

"Sorry."

"You're no use to me half asleep, you know. When we're out on a job you keep your wits about you, right? Right."

But when one non-working afternoon Janice

came home with pale yellow streaks banded into the front of her brownish hair Grace lost her temper. "For God's sake, Jan, what've you done to yourself?"

Janice's bloom faded. "I had it streaked."

"I can see that, can't I? What'd you do it for?"

"It's cool. It makes me look, you know, elegant . . ."

"Elegant! You look like a tabby cat in a rain storm. Next thing you'll be dying it pink like all them punks. You're too old for that lark, my girl."

Janice said sulkily, "I like it. It brightens me up. I'm sick of being that draggy old brown."

"So what does your boyfriend think of it?"

"Who?"

"Come off it, Jan, I'm not stupid. You'd only make a sight of yourself like that for a man."

Janice turned away. "He's not seen it yet."

"I bet he throws a fit. What's his name?"

"Dave."

"Dave what?"

"I don't know."

"Don't people have no surnames these days? What does he do?"

"He's in the post office."

"Doing what?"

"I don't know."

"You don't know much, do you. Are you seeing him regular?"

"Sort of. Sometimes he don't show."

Grace got up and fetched cigarettes from her handbag on the table. She lit one and blew the smoke out slowly.

"Listen to me, Jan. What you do in your own time's your own affair. But anything affecting our business arrangements that's different. I don't want you seeing no one regular. And I don't want those streaks in your hair neither."

"But . . ."

Grace held up her hand. "See someone regular and they're on to you, right? You can't help but let out little bits of this and that, like where you work or where you're from. The great thing about you and me as a team is that we're both on our own. No family, no strings. We're anonymous. And that's why those streaks of yours have got to go. They're memorable. Some old dear can't remember much but she can remember one of the ladies had yellow streaks in her hair. I want them out, Jan, and back to your old draggy brown before next week."

"I don't see . . ."

"Yes you do, dear. You're not as silly as that. Or if you are then it's time you and me split up." She went to the kitchen alcove and filled the kettle. Over the sound of the water she said, "If that's what you want, you've only to say. Of course, I don't know where you'd go. Maybe this Dave of yours would take you on." She set two mugs on the tray, tea-bags, sugar and milk. Janice sat sullenly by the window, winding a streaked lock round her fingers.

The kettle boiled. Grace made the tea and brought it to the table. "It's up to you, Jan."

He stood her up again that evening, but the next night he was there. "Sorry about that. Duty called."

She felt literally sick with pleasure at the sight of him. Goodness knows why, he was just a fella. But he was so clean. Most fellas were scruffy, dirty old trainers, anoraks looking like they came out of Oxfam. Don't shave, smell of beer and armpits. Not Dave. Old Spice and his hair just the right length. His teeth were nice too, and his hands — hands you wouldn't feel made you dirty going into you.

Except he didn't seem interested. She could never be sure he would keep a date. When he did he bought her a drink, took her to a meal, teased her, gave her a squeeze and a pat before she got out of the car at the corner of her road, said "Seeya" and drove off. It made her wild. What was wrong with her? What was wrong with him?

Like all passive people, she was extremely obstinate, and the fact that his interest in her was less than hers in him only made her more persistent. When they got to her road this evening she did not get out but turned and put her arms round him and sank herself into his mouth in the way she had learned but never wanted to do before.

After an instant he responded. They slid down a bit in the seats, awkwardly over the gear lever. She put her hand on his fly; what she found there was satisfactory.

She whispered, "Can't we go to your place?"

"Not on, love."

"In the back, then?"

"Not here." They drew apart.

She had an awful thought. "You're not gay, are you?"

He put her hand back on his fly. "What do you think?"

They drove without speaking to the car park at the bottom of Hampstead Heath. The back of the Volkswagen was unhelpful, but sufficed.

"You're a funny kid," he said afterwards, turning the key in the ignition.

"You turn me on," she said simply.

He laughed, but a little uneasily. "You want

to watch it. Some fellas would run a mile, say a thing like that to them."

"Yeah."

The car stopped at the corner of her road. "Shall I see you, Dave?"

"I reckon."

"Honest?"

"Honest. Bar accidents."

He put his arm round her and kissed her gently; then pushed the hair back from her pale cheeks and kissed her again. "You're a real wally, you are. A real wally."

She got out and closed the door. He tooted the horn and drove off, and she walked home, dreamily.

4

Grace noted that the yellow streaks had vanished from Janice's hair and therefore refrained from pursuing the subject of the boyfriend — he would drift away, as they all did, or Janice herself did, before very long. She was perfectly confident of her control over Janice, and just at the moment it quite suited her that Janice should be elsewhere on a Sunday evening and not tagging along with Grace, as had been their custom when they first set up together.

In those first few weeks in the miserable room at King's Cross they had fallen into the habit of spending Sunday evenings at a handsome public house near Tottenham Court Road, only a few stops on the Underground. There were several bars of various kinds, and while Grace preferred the murky homeliness of one, with its red banquettes and octagonal-topped tables, Janice could trail off to a livelier section, with flashing prismatic lights, space invaders and

74

one-armed bandits, a more dominating Muzak of thudding beat.

Grace would remain on the banquette till ten o'clock, making one drink last, neat in her navy two-piece and raincoat, her gingery waves released from a chiffon scarf, her make-up in no way noticeable. The warmth, the subdued lighting, the murmuring voices and laughter, the grossly patterned carpet beneath her sensible shoes, the sound of music issuing faintly from the ceiling, all merged into a palatable shepherd's pie of an atmosphere in which she felt at home — a less raucous NAAFI.

The clientele was mainly casual, for this was London's West End; but there were several regulars with whom, after a week or so, she had exchanged a cool nod and a good evening — nothing more, she was not there to make contacts but just for relaxation, a night out. There were one or two couples, a highly coloured middle-aged woman who spent her time up at the bar with the men, and a solitary elderly man who always sat by himself in the same corner, giving a civil response to any greeting but otherwise withdrawn. He was a large man, weighty and silent, balding, in a good blue suit with toning shirt and tie. He was always there when Grace and Janice arrived and always left before they did, sharp on half-past nine, and in that time had consumed a bottle of medium-priced burgundy. It was this which had caught Grace's attention in a place where beer or spirits were the usual tipple. He drank reflectively, sitting four-square on the plastic leather banquette, separate from but not opposed to the convivial hurly-burly around him. Grace too always chose a banquette if there were room, for she liked to have her back covered and a clear view of whatever room she was in. Janice had hardly been aware of him, but Grace had noted the good suit, the well-shaved jowls, the signet ring on his large hand.

Grace travelled the gusty tunnels of the Northern line on her own that Sunday evening to emerge in central London and enter the pub. She obtained her drink and took it to the table near where he sat. They exchanged a nod but nothing more. It was a mild May evening and the bar not full; there was no one on the banquette between them. She sipped her gin and vermouth and seemed lost in thought.

At long last he said, "Pleasant evening."

She seemed startled from her reverie. "Oh — yes it is. Soon be summer."

"If we get any."

"Fearful last year, wasn't it? The garden was washed out."

"Fortunately I don't have a garden."

"Ah." They drank, she in dainty sips, he in a long swallow. "Live in London, do you?"

"Notting Hill."

"That'd be the Central line."

"That's right. And you?"

"Belsize Park. The Northern."

"Yes."

Silence again, while around them Muzak and laughter hummed.

At half-past nine he got to his feet, nodded. "Well, good-night."

She smiled coolly. "Good night."

He left.

The next Sunday, to Grace's annoyance, Janice was with her, moping because her Dave was on shift. She didn't even go coasting up at the bar but just sat beside Grace with a face like a wet weekend. Good evenings were passed between Grace and the stolid gentleman but no conversation; Janice was enough to put anyone off. He emptied the bottle and left at half-past nine, saying good night.

But the following Sunday Grace was on her own again and judged it time to advance a cautious step. After the nod and the greeting, the first sip of her drink, she said,

"Disappointing, the weather."

His stolidity relaxed slightly. "Yes. Too good to last, I suppose."

"When I saw it coming down like that, I nearly didn't come out."

"Ah."

"Then I thought, no, I won't let a bit of rain stop me. It does you good to get out."

"Yes."

A pause, sipping.

"My niece — that's who you saw me with — she's gone out with her boyfriend this evening. But of course, he's got a car."

"They're a convenience."

"More trouble than they're worth in London, though, don't you think? Parking and the price of petrol always going up. I prefer London Transport."

"It's a good system. People grumble, but it's a good system."

"People grumble about everything these days, don't they."

"We're a nation of grumblers, if you ask me."

"That's very true." He refilled his glass; then, his large face uneasily jovial, said, "Can I get you another?"

"Well — that's very kind. I don't usually take more than the one."

"I know."

She looked at him sharply and to her surprise saw a glint of liveliness in his pale grey eyes. She allowed herself a smile and said, "It's a gin and vermouth, thanks."

Thereafter if conversation did not exactly flow it at least moved. The subjects were general; she found out nothing at all about him and was far too clever to probe. She told him equally nothing about herself, and what little she did was, naturally, false by implication. She did not define her own status, for she knew that nothing frightens a certain kind of man more than a widow; nor did he define his, although she gathered he was coming up to retirement from some large organisation. Since he was always alone he was presumably unmarried; retirement age and therefore due for a pension, no doubt a good one, since he seemed to have been with the company for many years and his clothes and his bottles of burgundy were not cheap. She surmised him to be a widower of some long time, set in his ways and selfish, living in a block of flats put up in the 1930s, with a woman to do the shopping and clean three days a week, cooking his own meals and making no mess, with a hobby perhaps like stamps or old coins.

When half-past nine came she left the Old George with him, hurrying together through the rain to Tottenham Court Road station under his man's umbrella, huge as a howdah, to shake hands formally at the foot of the escalator and go their separate ways to Northern and to Central lines. Grace was satisfied with the evening, and with the new scheme that was taking shape in her mind.

For Grace was never one to stand still. You had to look to the future, be flexible, especially if you wanted to keep ahead of the Old Bill. And she was increasingly aware that, although Janice had obeyed her about the streaked hair, she must still be seeing that Dave, for she had gone quite peculiar. She had always been dreamy but lately she was almost half-witted. Like last Wednesday . . .

They had been working West Hampstead, the grey terraces that drop down to Kilburn, colourful only in their mixed population and the grafitti on their sometimes derelict walls. Down three steps to a half-basement, a window-box full of straggling mint and chives, a curling visiting-card tacked above a bell-push — useful in giving a name.

The door was opened cautiously. Grace put on her smile. "Miss Greenham?"

It was swung open and a joyful but anxious-faced Miss Greenham reached out and pulled her inside. "You've come!" she cried, then peered at Janice. "Two of you?"

"This is Mary, my assistant."

"Miss Pennyquick, yes? Come in, dear, quickly, before they spot us."

Janice stepped into the passageway, now impenetrably dark as Miss Greenham closed and bolted the front door. "I don't when I'm alone for they don't know about me, but now you're here we must be on our guard." She pressed past them down the passage. "We'd best go in the back, we're not overlooked there. And the TV's in the front."

Nothing surprised Grace. They followed the old lady into the kitchen, cluttered and close because the curtains were drawn, smelling of what Janice at first thought was pot but was in fact herbal tea.

"Sit down, sit down," cried Miss Greenham. "How good of them to send you so quickly!"

She was a large woman; usually Grace liked them small — just in case something went wrong, but at the post office the day before (apparently filling out a renewal of car licence form while studying the queue of old dears drawing their pensions) she had noted the pebble lenses on the broad face, the stick and the bandaged leg. She had noticed too that four weeks' pension, not one, was being drawn and she had followed the limping old lady home with optimism.

Now she sat down at the table, on which a number of pamphlets and old copies of the

Guardian were scattered alongside a bowl full of bean sprouts and a half empty jar of chutney, and opened her briefcase. "I'm Mrs. Black from the DHSS . . ."

"No need, no need," said Miss Greenham, "no need for subterfuge! We're quite safe here. The front room's different, even though I keep the TV covered with a blanket — it's the videos, you know, next door. They pick up everything, even when they're not switched on, so that's why I brought you in here." She sank into the one armchair, against which a walking-stick leaned.

"It's very cosy," Grace said.

"It's *safe,*" said Miss Greenham, "that's the main thing. When I wrote to the Home Secretary I told him my back room is quite *safe,* he need not fear his people would be in any danger here."

"No?" Grace offered. Janice, who had sat down in a chair near the gas cooker, was gaping like a half-wit.

"No," said Miss Greenham, "I wouldn't risk the life of one of Her Majesty's agents for anything in the world, let alone two." She beamed at Janice, who managed to smile back. "It's so good of him to send you so quickly. The matter is urgent. They don't suspect that I know but I overhear them, you see, especially at night. It's the poor black people they're after, them and the IRA — I mean them and the IRA are after the black people here and will stop at nothing, absolutely nothing. And they're so hard-working and good, open all hours, even Sundays, and as for the others, London Transport would come to a standstill if they had their way. But of course you know all this."

Grace nodded. There was a very nice pair of silver candlesticks on the mantelshelf over the gas fire, and two nice china figures on either side of them. And Miss Greenham's handbag bulged on the floor beside her walking-stick.

"But what you and the Home Secretary don't know," continued Miss Greenham in a lower voice, "is that there is this conspiracy to send them all home. Why do you think Freddie Laker went bust? Because he refused to take them. And Mr. De Lorean — such a handsome man — they wanted to use his vehicles. And dear Mr. Heseltine, the helicopters."

"Well I never," said Grace.

"Yes." She sat back. "I thought that would surprise you. And that's not all . . ." Miss Greenham's large face, with its bridge of pebble lenses and Afro of thin white hair, grew pink with excitement over the next ten minutes as Grace sat listening quietly (but rezipped her briefcase, documents not needed) and Janice, she noticed, sank into a dream.

When at last Miss Greenham paused Grace said, "This is all ever so valuable, dear. I'll see the information goes right back to the proper authorities, they'll be ever so grateful."

"It's for the Commonwealth," said Miss Greenham simply.

"That's right, dear. I only wish more people felt like you do." She smiled her smile. "Would you like Mary to make us a cup of tea now? You must be ever so dry after all that talking."

"Of course, of course . . ." Miss Greenham surged up, but Grace gestured her back.

"No, no, Mary will make it, won't you, Mary? You go on with your story, dear."

"There's camomile or verbena. On the shelf . . ."

"Yes, yes, Mary'll find it." She glanced at Janice, who had got to her feet and was filling the kettle. "Go on with what you were telling me . . ."

Janice stood waiting for the kettle to boil, gazing out through a chink in the curtains to the weed-rich garden beyond. She thought about Dave. She thought about the way his hair grew, about his smell. She thought about how they fitted themselves into the small back of his car and she tried so hard to make it right for him; how he'd said it was but she wasn't sure, although she *was* sure because men couldn't fake it like girls could. She thought about his voice and the way he teased her, but always gently like as if he was fond of her really. He called her "love" as if he meant it, and when he kissed her, he was kissing *her*, not just slobbering a piece of meat like some of them. Yet even in the back of the car she had the feeling he was only half there. He never came out with anything — not where he lived, where he worked. He teased and smiled and was gentle, listened to the lies she told him about herself as though amused by them. Asked nothing, gave nothing except what she had almost nagged from him by her doting persistence. A fella'd have to be mad to refuse what was owed, mad or gay and Dave wasn't either. He was just — unobtainable, even when they were screwing.

The kettle boiled and, still in a dream, she put the sachets of what was marked "verbena" (surely "camomile" was a shampoo?) into the cups and squeezed them with a spoon; then, shielding them from the room as she had been trained to do, reached into the pocket of her jeans for the Sweetex tube in which she always carried the powdered sleeping pills . . . Dave never took sugar, teased it would make her fat, never drank beer only lager, and his body (her own gave a lurch in its most hidden place as she thought of it) was hard and springy with a special sexy smell . . . The top of the tube came off suddenly and she spilled the whole contents all over the draining-board . . .

Grace had seen, had got up and taken the tray from her, had spooned the spilt powder into a cup and placed the tray on the table. With perfect composure she had told Janice to sit and drink while she, with steady hand and eyes like ice, mopped up and rinsed away the rest of their only profit-making means of operation, the small white drift of powder in the sink and on the mouldering wood of Miss Greenham's draining-board. "Drink it all up, Mary," she said, leaving her own untouched, while Miss Greenham drank up her nauseous brew, explaining the aims of the National Front and sending messages to the Home Secretary and the head of MI5.

"You bloody silly bitch!" hissed Grace as they went up the road towards the Underground. "You nearly cocked the whole thing up! What d'you think you are, Sleeping Beauty?"

"I couldn't help it, my hand slipped."

"Hand slipped! Half the stuff down the drain, you silly cow, hardly enough left to do the job! It's a bloody miracle she went off like she did."

The hold-alls were nevertheless satisfactorily heavy, the china figures wrapped in a nice silk blouse, the candlesticks in a fur cape strong with mothballs.

"Get out of my sight, Jan. Piss off. I don't want to lay eyes on you till I've calmed down."

They parted. Grace seldom used bad language and when she did Janice knew better than to stick around.

Yes, Grace was coming to the end of Janice. Which would mean the end of this particular means of livelihood, for although it would be possible to work it alone it would be more risky. Apart from the fact that two women on a doorstep were more reassuring than one, there were the actual mechanics to be considered: it would be difficult to slip the powder into the cup without even the doziest old thing noticing if there were not a second person talking away and distracting attention. And one person alone could hardly carry away the larger acquisitions, like clocks and radios and good pairs of shoes. You needed the two.

Besides which, it was Janice who got the sleeping pills, prescribed by a ramshackle medical group after she came out of prison and renewed automatically on request ever since. Grace could no doubt have found her own supplies, but Janice was safer and more convenient.

No, if Janice were discarded, so must this scheme be. It had served very well — three months of nice pickings and never so much as a whisper of the Old Bill. Hard to see how they could ever get on to it, unless they were lucky enough to pick up something that she'd sold and trace it back to her, and that was very unlikely. With larceny or shop-lifting or any fiddle to do with form-filling and claims for this and that you were up against people often as sharp as you were; but with old folk you were home and dry. Trusting as babies they were, with their bad sight, bad legs, bad hearing and, most of all, their awe of official-dom.

Grace had learned all this in the old people's homes. She had gone in as a domestic in a blue overall but her well-spoken composure had soon upgraded her to a white one and charge of the inmates — not medically, of course, for she could not produce qualifica-tions, but even so there were times when she took round the drug trolley; and it was here that she learned about dosages and the func-tions of this tablet or that. Stashed away a few, too, thinking they might come in handy one day . . .

She'd been soft with Janice. Something about the girl's sheer cluelessness had ap-pealed to her. God knows what would have happened to her when she came out if Grace hadn't taken her over, she had no more sense than a baby although she was nearly thirty. But (a faint echo from chapel services in prison) for all things there is a season and Janice's season was pretty well up. She had nearly blown it with Miss Greenham, who might have been on to them, pebble lenses or no pebble lenses, if she hadn't been nutty as a fruit cake, and if Grace hadn't acted so quickly. And those streaks in her hair and that Dave — who knew what the silly cow might do or let on to him, she seemed quite to have lost her marbles. Janice would have to go.

But not quite yet; not until Grace was ready. The new scheme that had come into Grace's mind was more ambitious than any she had ever tried before. It would need the most delicate handling and could not be hurried. Janice had no place in it. It was entirely up to Number One.

"What you putting that on for?" asked Janice, pausing in the varnishing of her toenails. Her hair, lightened but no longer streaked, hung over her face, which, in the twilight of this late May Sunday, looked much younger than her years; since Dave she had acquired a vulnerable look, bemused rather than inert, which gave her an almost childlike air if the light and her make-up were right.

"Never you mind," said Grace. Her months in the old folks' homes had made her adept with bandages and she wound the pink crepe deftly round her ankle and fastened it with a neat reef-knot.

"You'll stop your circulation," said Janice, returning to her toes.

"I've got more sense than that." She stretched her leg out and surveyed the bandaged ankle. Satisfied, she rolled on her stocking and made ready to leave. "You going out?"

"Yeah."

"Don't forget to lock up then." Janice was so dozey she sometimes forgot to lock the door to their room, and with a house full of anonymous and no doubt transient lodgers there was no knowing what thieves might be about.

Although it was not raining Grace extracted an umbrella from the dusty collection no one ever noticed in a corner of the communal hall, and walked briskly to the Underground.

At the door of the Old George saloon bar she paused. It was half empty, for the evening was fine and the Muzak was blandly audible above a mere murmur of conversation from the few people at the bar. Mr. Robinson (they had exchanged names by now) was sitting in his accustomed place, the whole banquette empty beside him, the bottle of burgundy well broached. She thought (and hoped) that he was watching for her but, leaning heavily on the umbrella, she limped forward with a concentrated air as though it were all she could do to be moving at all, let alone recognise anyone.

As she made her way slowly towards the banquette he half rose to his feet, sloshing the wine in his glass, concern faintly evident on his large face.

"Well now, been in the wars?"

She gave him a brave smile while manoeuvring herself painfully down on to the seat beside him. She sat with a thump, getting her breath back, the umbrella resting at her side.

"My word!" She put a hand to her breast. "I never thought I'd make it!"

"What have you done to yourself?"

"I fell off a chair dusting the top of the wardrobe. Imagine! My foot just seemed to slip and down I came."

"It's not broken?"

"No, no, it's just a sprain. I can wiggle my toes all right." She smiled.

"You shouldn't have come out. Rest it, keep it up."

"Well, I enjoy my Sunday evenings here, the music and that. It makes a change."

"Let me get you a drink."

"That's ever so kind. I'm not sure I could make it to the bar." This time she laughed, raising a small smile from him. He was a lump and no mistake!

He returned with her gin and vermouth, a double. "Ooh, you shouldn't of. It'll go to my head!"

"Nonsense. Alcohol's good for sprains."

"On the outside, Mr. Robinson, not inside! I was a nurse long enough to know that! Anyway, cheers!"

"*Votre santé*" he responded ponderously. They drank.

The evening went very well. Her frailty loosened him up a little. She learned that he lived not as she had imagined but in an old-fashioned mansion flat and that he did his own cooking. She could not discover if he lived alone or not, delicately probe though she might; never mind, another time. He was something senior in a building society and knew about stocks and shares. He was due to retire next February. He went abroad every September for his holidays.

Of her he learned rather more: that she was a widow (a long sad illness, devotedly nursed) with a sufficient pension; that she had been a nurse before her marriage; that her niece (who was like a daughter to her) worked as a dentist's receptionist in Hampstead and would probably soon be getting married; after which Grace would look around for a little flat of her own, their present quarters being only temporary. She had learned over the years that offering detailed information about herself was the best way of getting it from others; it made them feel superior, that you were giving yourself away to them.

But it did not work very well with Mr. Robinson.

When half-past nine came he emptied his glass, buttoned his jacket and looked at her sidelong with a touch of uneasiness. "Well — time to be making tracks." He always said that.

"Yes, I must be moving too. It shakes you up a bit, a fall." Her own glass had been empty for some time.

"It's the shock."

"That's right. I wonder, Mr. Robinson, would you be ever so kind and try to catch me a taxi? I got a mini-cab down here, just couldn't face the tube. Taxis always stop easier for a man than for a lady."

"Certainly, certainly. Here, let me . . ." He got to his feet and moved the table away so that she was able, with the aid of the umbrella, to stand up, wincing a little as she put her weight on the bandaged ankle. "Take my arm."

Gratefully she did so. It was like a log of wood.

There were plenty of taxis and one stopped at once at the command of Mr. Robinson's large hand.

"Belsize Park," she told the driver, and to Mr. Robinson, "Thanks ever so much, you've been so kind."

"Will you be all right?"

"Don't worry about me."

"Mind how you go, then."

"I will." She got herself into the taxi and he shut the door. She smiled and waved at him as the taxi turned away. When he was out of sight she leaned forward and opened the driver's glass partition. "Goodge Street Underground," she said, and sat back well satisfied.

The following Sunday evening she still limped a little and leaned on the umbrella but had left the bandage off.

"Was that wise?" he asked as she sat down beside him, her leg gracefully stretched out beneath the table.

"I can't bear to cosset myself. Face up to things, I always say. It's only when I put my weight on it I feel it now."

"You'll have your usual?"

She demurred but he went off, quite eager.

When Janice, moping because her Dave was on shift this Sunday, had said she'd come too, Grace had cut her off. "No thanks, you're not wanted."

"Huh?"

"You mind your business, I'll mind mine. We're not in each other's pockets."

Janice had been huffy, but Grace had been right. He was almost chatty, and she ventured a next move.

"I wonder," she said delicately, in a pause after a conversation about the prospects for Wimbledon, "I wonder, while the weather's nice, if you'd care to come to tea with me and my niece one Sunday?" He blenched but she continued, "We've got the garden flat and it's nice to sit out in the patio when the weather's fine. We'd be ever so pleased to see you."

He huffed and puffed before saying it was kind of her but he didn't think . . . He wasn't one for travelling far afield, not on a Sunday. . . . He kept a regular routine, certain jobs in the flat kept him busy, accounts, shopping and so on. . . .

She helped him. "I quite understand," she said. And she did. She had gambled on just such a response, guessed to a word just what his excuses would be. If by any chance she had been wrong and he had accepted it would have been easy enough to cry off at the last minute with illness, or Janice absent, or herself called away by an ailing friend. "I quite understand," she repeated, "I'm the same myself."

She accepted serenely his departure slightly earlier than usual, for she knew she had ruffled him a little. And she did not go to the Old George the following Sunday. Give him time for his alarm to die down, to miss their meeting a little.

Grace was seldom wrong about these things, and when she appeared again a fortnight later he was clearly pleased to see her. And the week after that he suggested they have a bite together instead of staying in the bar. He took her to a steak house whose subdued lighting and crimson decor mimicked the gravy and red meat put before them; even the air seemed cooked. He drank most of a bottle of Beaujolais without the least effect.

But try as she might, in the most discreetly womanly of ways, revealing little tidbits of her own past (much of it sad and none of it true) she learned hardly anything of his own. He had been with the building society ever since he came out of the army after doing his national service. That he was domesticated was plain, for he knew about food and how it should be cooked and sent his steak back to the kitchen because it was not just as he liked it. "I expect to get what I pay for," he said with a glimmer of a smile. He seldom smiled and never laughed, keeping a ponderous impassivity which suited his bulk and the old-fashioned courtesy of his behaviour — he held umbrellas and doors open, helped on with coats, half got to his feet when she approached or left to go to the ladies. He certainly knew how to treat women yet there was no hint that he had ever been married.

He might, of course, be gay — you never could be sure nowadays; but Grace's instincts told her he was not. He might be a long-time widower, in circumstances that had left a scar. He was certainly not sexy; Grace would not have embarked on him if he had been sexy, that sort were too much trouble. As it was, she was as genteel as he, womanly but ladylike, nothing to frighten him in any way.

It was the first time she had ever engaged in this sort of scheme but she was confident of her skill; here she was, after little more than six weeks and what you could call a casual pick-up, sitting in a steak house with this gentlemanly fellow with his good suit and gold wristwatch and not one to choose the cheapest dish or leave too small a tip. He was coming along nicely.

Sure enough, the invitation was repeated the

next Sunday. And as they finished their coffee and he signalled for the bill he said offhandedly, "I wonder if, next Sunday, you'd care to take tea at my place? My mother would be pleased to meet you."

Inwardly Grace reeled. A mother! She kept her customary pleasant smile. "That's very kind. Does she live near you?"

"We live together."

All she could summon up was "Oh."

When Janice noticed that Grace was getting ready to go out that Sunday afternoon she stared up from the women's magazine on her lap and said, "You going out already?"

Snapping on plain stud earrings, Grace answered, "That's right."

"Where you going?" For it was unheard of for Grace to go out on a Sunday until the jaunt to the Old George in the evening. Sunday was a do-nothing day, slopping about in dressing-gowns, drinking coffee, having the radio on but not really to listen. At mid-day Grace would cook a big fry-up and then, with the *A* to *Z* street guide, plan the next week's operations. Janice would snooze, do her nails, try out new hair-styles she never kept, restlessly waiting for the time to pass until she could get ready for Dave, dress up, do her face, perfume, rush from the house (although she was always early) and wait at their usual place for him to come. Sometimes he didn't; sometimes he just stood her up and it made her mad, but mad in a sad way. Anyone else she would have told to piss off, would have looked around for someone else. But she didn't want anyone else — those overweight, sweaty, boozy men who called her "Darling" and tried a quick feel. She had hardly noticed them and what they were up to in the past, accepting them simply as a means of staying alive. Now the thought of them made her sick.

She would have gone to a call-box and telephoned him but he'd never given her a number. "Don't call us, we'll call you," he had joked early on; but he never had — there was a pay phone in the hall of their lodgings, and when they were due to meet she always listened in case it rang and was him. But it never was.

She fretted. She wondered all the time where was he, who was he with? Had he someone else as well? Yet when he was with her, when, after a missed date, he did turn up, he was always gentle. "Sorry, love," he'd say and kiss her, "it was panic-stations, an emergency. Just couldn't make it." And she'd melt.

So she moped through Sundays but hid it from Grace, for after Grace's strictures about never making contacts that might lead back she was afraid of Grace.

Now, as she always did, Grace answered, "Ask no questions and you'll hear no lies." She smoothed her eyebrows with a moistened forefinger, turning her head appraisingly in front of the mirror, applied a discreetly rosy lipstick.

Janice giggled. "Are you out on the tiles, then?"

Grace gave her a cold look. "I've said it before and I'll say it again. You mind your business and I'll mind mine." She tied a chiffon scarf lightly under her chin, picked up her handbag. "I suppose you'll be out when I get back. Don't wake me if you're late."

Well! It took Janice's mind off Dave for a while, for she knew Grace had no more interest in sex than a cod in the deep freeze. She must be up to something. Would it include Janice? And if it didn't, what would become of her? She'd be out on her own again, helpless, unless Dave . . .

Later, in a leafy cul-de-sac near Hampstead Heath, as they tidied themselves up a bit afterwards in the cramped back of the car, she began to cry. She cried and cried and her mascara ran and she looked like a bedraggled teenager. He wiped her cheeks gently with the heel of his hand. "Hey, hey, what's up?"

"I know I'm no good."

"What you on about?"

"I don't turn you on."

"What d'you think we've just been doing?"

"I'm no good."

He put the wet hair back from her face. "You didn't get there, did you?"

"Where?"

"Where, she says! Where you ought to be on such occasions." He kissed her cheek. "You're an insult to my manhood, you are."

Her sobs had diminished; she was only snivelling now, blowing her nose and reaching round for her handbag. "I'm sorry. I know I'm no good."

"Why d'you always think so little of yourself?"

"I make a mess of everything."

"Sure you do." He laughed and gave her a squeeze. "And d'you know why? Because you expect to. You want to get hold of yourself, love, think big, act positive."

"Oh, Dave . . ."

"Why don't you get a job? There's plenty around if you're not fussy. Drifting around like a jellyfish all day does you no good."

"I don't . . ."

"Yeah, yeah, modelling, receptioning, all that glitz. I mean a real job, nine to five, in a shop or an office or something. The puritan work ethic."

At her uncomprehending stare he laughed and kissed her again. "You're a wally, you are! Come on, let's get moving."

When he dropped her off as usual at the corner of her road she asked fearfully, "Will I see you again?"

"Sure — but not till Friday, okay? I'm on nights."

"It was all right, then?"

"Look, Jan," he took her hand, "give it a rest, will you? Sex is simpler for boys than girls and I've no complaints. But your education's been neglected."

"What?"

He laughed and opened the car door. "Go on, go home. I'll see you Friday."

She got out. With a slam of the door and a wave he drove off. She watched till he turned the corner out of sight, then walked slowly home, as bemused as ever but with a timid joy deep inside her. She didn't know what he was on about but he did seem to care, just a bit. She wasn't a dead loss.

Notting Hill Gate was not an area Grace knew well. The workmen's cottages that lay behind the Coronet cinema had long ago become smart little town houses with carriage lamps and window boxes and glossy front doors, while beyond them, towards Kensington as well as to the north towards Westbourne Grove, the houses had always been large and prosperous, not lived in by the kind of people Grace needed. Beyond that again, around the Harrow Road, where endless rows of run-down terrace houses used to be, there were now mostly huge blocks of council flats; except for the ground floors, where old folk tended to live, Grace did not care to work the council blocks — too many watching windows, too many staircases and narrow walkways to get lost in. In any case, she preferred to work along the Northern line and its many interchanges; it was more convenient.

So she was glad that Mr. Robinson had offered to meet her at Notting Hill Underground and escort her to his home; it showed he was a gentleman and saved her the trouble of finding her own way. He stood by the ticket collector, solid in his customary dark suit, and shook her hand formally when she came through the barrier.

"No trouble getting here?"

"No, easy as pie. I had to wait ever such a long time for a train, though."

"Sunday service."

"Weekdays aren't much better. Not that I travel much."

"This way."

It was a big, old-fashioned block of mansion flats to which they walked, nothing at all like the 1930s honeycomb she had envisaged. She kept her composure well, just as she had when he had first announced he had a mother, and what's more, lived with her. She had been flabbergasted at first but satisfaction had soon followed, for it was good that the mother wished to meet his friend, and, heaven knows, Grace was used to old people. There was nothing she didn't know about their little ways nor how to keep the old dears happy. She would not deny that the news had given her a shock at first; she had been so confident of her reading of his situation, and a mother was totally unexpected. But it could turn out to be an advantage, for a sympathetic, mature female ear to the complaints of a lonely old woman would be just the job. Once Grace had won her over, Mr. Robinson would be that much easier.

The interior of the mansion block consisted of grey stone corridors and staircases, not unlike those in the Peabody Buildings tenements in which Grace had once, long ago, briefly lived. They did not mount but went along the ground-floor passage to a door at the end which Mr. Robinson opened with Yale and mortice keys, having first rung the bell three times and rattled the letterbox.

They entered a long dark passage in which several doors stood closed and whose walls were crammed with photographs or pictures. At the end a door was half-open and from it a breath of heat flavoured with peppermint met them.

Mr. Robinson went in, "It's us, Mother."

"Ah. Well met."

The voice was not that of a little old lady with cataract and a bad heart but of a stately matron almost as large, although seated in a wing chair, as her son. She was stout rather than fit, the flesh packed into a commanding bosom over which a number of chains and necklaces lay like offerings on an altar, and massive arms revealed in an almost sleeveless dress of royal blue. That she was tall was evident, for her head topped the back of the throne-like chair. Although the room was dusky (french windows on to a small, high-walled yard did not let in much light, being hung with muslin and brocade) Grace could see that Mrs. Robinson's hair was so determined a black as to be almost green, styled in the mode of Mrs. Thatcher. It surmounted a face as fleshy and square-jawed as that of her son but with a higher colour, a lipsticked mouth and eye shadow of turquoise blue. Large pearl studs were on her ear lobes, a heavy ring or two on her big hands, which rested on either chair-arm like those of a monarch.

"Well met," she repeated in a rich voice, "Mrs. — er . . ."

"Black," said Grace. She had intended, at this stage of introduction to the supposed old dear, to say, "But call me Grace." But not now.

"Conroy, draw up a chair."

He did so and Grace sat down, holding her handbag on her lap. The room was very hot, with the central section of an old-fashioned gas fire rasping out from a green-tiled fireplace. It was full of furniture as massively padded as its mistress and, as in the passage, the walls were close-packed with pictures and what, out of the corner of her eye, looked to Grace like certificates.

Mrs. Robinson studied her for a moment, from her sensible court shoes up to her discreet make-up and well-tinted hair. "It's so nice of you to come," she said at last. "Conroy is such a secretive fellow, he's told me almost nothing about you."

Behind Grace's smile her mind was going clunk-clunk-clunk as it adapted to a complete change of circumstance. She said modestly, "There's really nothing to tell."

"There is always something to tell! Every human being is a treasury of thought and emotion. You're a widow, I believe?"

"That's right."

"I too — but you know that, of course. I'm fortunate to have so good a son, he's such a staunch companion. You have no children?"

"No. I've always regretted it. The war was on and my hubby was overseas and then soon after he was demobbed. . . ." She gave a sad smile. "But I've got my niece — I'm sure Mr. Robinson's told you. It's not the same, of course, but she's a good girl. She'd always look after me."

"That's what one needs to know, isn't it? To know one will be looked after."

Grace shifted her chair a little from the fire, for she could feel her face begining to colour up and her body becoming uncomfortably hot in a way which interfered with her clarity of thought. She was aware that Mr. Robinson (Conroy!) had disappeared, and from what must be the kitchen came the sound of crockery being placed, drawers opened and shut.

"Do you know this part of London, Mrs. Black? It's changed a great deal, of course. The old Notting Hill has quite vanished, all the little shops and now these hideous modern buildings put in their place. Of course there used to be a lot of slums, quite rough, I believe. But the area had character, you know, much more than now it's been smartened up — gentrified, I believe is the term."

As she spoke her son brought in a tray covered with a lace-edged cloth and laden with tea things. He put it down on the small table beside his mother's chair, went back to the kitchen and returned with an old-fashioned cake stand, every tier bearing a plate of delicacies.

"Thank you, dear," said his mother, and twisted her large body round to pour the tea. "Milk? And sugar?" The cup was passed. "Do have a sandwich — Conroy's an expert at sandwiches, I don't know how he gets the bread so thin."

As the pleasantries continued Grace's mind was working double-quick time. There was Robinson himself to be reassessed; could he after all be gay? Nancyboys were always tied to their mother's apron-strings and this old cow in front of her (she must be eighty if a day, for Conroy — Conroy! — had said he was due for retirement soon) certainly had some apron-strings! If he were — but that need not be bad. Nancys like women friends, and if he went for the motherly type then Grace could be ever so motherly when she wanted. But somehow she didn't believe he was. There was something too stolid and obstinate about him, despite his dainty sandwiches. In which case . . . But Mum had to be reckoned with. Mum, as the Yanks had it, was a whole new ball game.

Grace, keeping her pleasant smile in place, studied her hostess. She was still a handsome woman, with a skin remarkably smooth for someone of her age, although nothing could hide the sags and wrinkles of her neck nor the flab of her arms, which it would have been better to cover with long sleeves. Her make-up was old-fashioned, overcoloured in the way that would have been stylish when she was in her prime and now, Grace felt, rather disgusting on an old biddy. Her black hair was, frankly, ridiculous.

Letting her gaze drop demurely as she sipped her tea, she saw that Mrs. Robinson's legs were huge and wrapped around with bandages. Grace knew that meant ulcers, varicose veins gone bad, and probably high blood pressure — she'd seen it often enough in the old folks' homes. That meant she wasn't able to get about. Right. Now we know a bit more just where we are . . .

"I see you're looking at my pictures," Mrs. Robinson said when the small talk was running out, "my treasures." She looked round the room with satisfaction. "I was in the theatre, you know, as I expect Conroy has told you." Grace shook her head. Mrs. Robinson sent her son a playful (or was it baleful?) glance. "Ah, funny boy! He's always been self-conscious about having a famous mother. Well, perhaps not famous . . ." She simpered. "But not totally unknown. I was Marion Conroy."

"Ah."

"I see you don't remember." She gave Grace a sharp look. "Perhaps you don't listen to the wireless?"

"Not very much, no. I . . ."

"I was Lady Belhampton in 'Nanny Jane's Journal.'"

That did mean something to Grace; even if you never listened to it, everyone had known of the bi-weekly radio serial about life in a great house in Queen Victoria's time. It had started soon after the war and run till a few years ago; the old dears in the home had loved it, those that could still love anything. "Well I never!" she said.

Mrs. Robinson was gratified. "Of course before that I was in the theatre proper — Stratford, the Old Vic. I gave it up when I married and Conroy came along — that explains his unusual Christian name, doesn't it? I wanted my stage career not to be quite forgotten." She gave her son another playful glance. "But then, when my husband died so tragically early — only fifty-three — I went back. I was in quite a number of West End plays — you may have seen some of the Salt and Pepper comedies at the Strand?"

Yes, Grace had. Bill Salt and Fay Pepper were a husband-and-wife comedy team who had put on a succession of farces in the fifties and early sixties and Grace had been to several during one of her spells in London. There was always a dignified middle-aged duchess sort of character in them that Salt and Pepper tried to score off but never quite did. Could that have been Mrs. Robinson?

It was. Conroy obediently took some of the framed photographs from the wall and Grace could verify the stage sets, the frozen comic postures, the inscriptions: To Marion, yours ever — Bill; Marion darling — kisses, Fay.

"Well I never!" she repeated.

There were also signed photographs of many other known and unknown theatre people, and what she had thought were certificates were framed theatre posters with MARION CONROY in medium-sized type below the play's titles. And there were books of press cuttings, smelling of mould, which Conroy lugged from the bottom shelves of a bookcase at his mother's command. "And next time you come I must show you my

111

costumes. Yes, I managed to keep one or two of the lovelier ones, the management was very good about that if you really longed for one and were one of the principals. And of course one's personal things — the jewels I wore as Regan, for instance — darling Donald always admired them so — and wigs, I always insisted on my own wigs."

During all this Conroy said very little, fetching and carrying and taking the tea things out into the kitchen. Grace had offered to wash up but he had brusquely refused, while his mother opened yet another album of cuttings across her massive lap. The era of "Nanny Jane's Journal" and the Salt and Pepper farces was vaguely recognisable to Grace but before that, back through strange names like Chekhov and Maugham, Old Vic and Gladys, she was lost. She looked at each page of yellowing clippings, making suitable exclamations, keeping an expression of genteel interest on her face, concealing a derisive amusement as the pictured Marion Conroy grew younger and younger in her old-time robes and tragic poses or all done up like a dog's dinner in satin evening dresses; or earlier still (during the First War, the dates were) in tights and tunic as, it said, Will Scarlett or flouncing in a shepherdess hat and blowing a kiss, not more than twenty, surely, and as bouncy a beauty as —

well, girls weren't like that any more, just look at Janice . . .

And here, on crumbling pages of something called *Play Pictorial* was a whole series of scenes taken at somewhere called the Stratford Memorial Theatre — the first Grace had heard of there being somewhere like that in the East End of London. Marion Conroy and the rest of them postured and stood like waxworks done up in sheets and old-time costumes, ever so serious and looking right daft. How could they keep straight faces?

Grace kept hers, and at last was able to gather herself together and depart. Mrs. Robinson lay back in her chair, replete with memories and looking her age — which Grace reckoned, having done some sums as the programmes and clippings dates passed by, must be well down her eighties. Her colour was high, seeming higher because of the jetty hair above, the smeared eye shadow and lipstick smudged out of shape, and her breathing was loud.

Conroy saw Grace to the front door but did not offer to escort her to the Underground. They parted with no future meeting mentioned and Grace walked back to Notting Hill Gate with a great deal to think about.

"How did it go, then? Your date?" Janice

remembered to ask next day. She had, as expected, been out when Grace returned, for which Grace was grateful: she had enough to think about without Janice mooning around.

"It was very nice."

"Did you go somewhere?"

"No. He's got a nice flat."

Janice did not question further for her curiosity, always slight, was lost in dreams of last evening's session in Dave's car. But a pang of envy pierced her that an old stick like Robinson should have a nice flat of his own to which to take his lady friends (not that Grace would get into that sort of thing) while Dave did not.

More and more often (although she tried not to in case he got pissed off with her) she found herself asking as they moved into the back seat in some back alley, or lay-by, "Why can't we go to your place, Dave?" They had got the hang of fitting themselves and it and each other, but although none of her past experiences had ever been on an actual bed she longed for a bed with Dave. Behind his teasing kindliness it was his sexual patience that was slowly making her aware that somewhere, behind, below, lurking, were responses, pulses, places just out of reach. She had never got anything more than a mild itch out of sex before, never really known what the men were on about. She let them have it because it was the currency for food and drink and a "good time"; and because it made her feel that, for the time it took, she was necessary to someone. But none of them had ever bothered to take more than the time it took or, once they got their flies unzipped, made her feel it was she, Janice, they were into rather than just a convenient hole.

Dave was different. He took trouble. A session with him in the back seat could take twenty minutes, with bits of her body not chewed up or banged about but alerting other bits, so that each time she was left with the feeling that somewhere ahead there waited something more, something by which her sluggish nature might be split and splintered like a rocket going off on Guy Fawkes' night.

But not cramped up in the back of the Volkswagen, half-clothed, expecting a policeman to shine his torch and have them up for indecent behaviour.

"Why can't we go to your place, Dave?"

"I've told you, love. My landlady won't have lady visitors."

"She'd be asleep."

"Ears like an elkhound." He was nibbling hers. "And a yappy dog."

"You could move."

"It suits me. She washes me briefs."

"What's the launderette for?" She pulled away crossly.

"For guys who've nothing better to do than sit there watching their smalls go round and chatting up the housewives." His hand went up under her sweater.

"Is she old?"

"Antique."

"You're not having it off with her?"

"You must be joking! You take all I've got."

"Do I, Dave?"

"Wanta bet?"

Nevertheless she never felt she really had him. He was patient and clever yet when it was over, although he held her and helped her do up her zips, she felt she had not got him. While it was happening he had been hers but now he had slipped away again, in the kiss on her cheek, the teasing about the crick in his back, the starting the car.

"Why can't we go to your place, Dave?"

It echoed in her head much of the time she was not with him — drifting about the room or looking in shops, going about with Grace on their working days. Not on the jobs themselves; she tried to concentrate while they were on the job, afraid of Grace's anger if anything was bungled again, going through the drill of tea-making and cup-loading while Grace did her spiel and spread her documents out and the old things lapped it up. But afterwards, in the Underground going home with their loaded carrier bags, the echoes came back: why can't we go to Dave's place, to lie down, stretch out, move up to, reach . . .

"Wake up, Jan, for Pete's sake! You're a proper zombie. . . ."

"Sorry, love, can't stop," said Dave, banging down on to the seat beside Janice at their next date; he was wearing his working clothes, jacket and slacks, not his off-duty casuals. "Slight panic on, not to worry, but it may be a day or so before I'm free." He patted her hand. "I'll meet you here Saturday, okay? It should have died down by then. And if it's blown over and you're a good girl we'll have a night out on the town. How's that?" He smoothed the hair back from her face, adding, "You've got the wrong eye shadow on again."

"What d'you mean, a night out?"

"A night out, wally! We'll go up west, stay in a hotel, have fun. Okay?"

Colour flushed up in her face. "You mean stay in a hotel?"

"Just said so, didn't I?"

"Oh, Dave!"

"I'll let you know Friday. If I'm here.

Should be by then. If not, keep trying, eh? See ya." He patted her hand again but she caught his and held it.

"Dave, d'you mean it? You're not having me on?"

"Would I do that, now? We'll fix it Friday, D.V."

"Oh, Dave!"

He kissed her quickly, got up and left. She sat bemused, suffused, forgetting her vodka and Coke. A whole night! In a hotel! In a bed . . .

The hotel where Dave had booked them had been built in nobler times in the heart of what was then the elegant West End and now was a mishmash of hamburger restaurants, strip clubs and curbside salesmen of every kind. Its lobby was high and vaulted, gilded and coloured sixty years ago and in need of re-touching, hung with chandeliers giving too weak a light. Where once, by the revolving doors, a commissionaire in livery had summoned taxis, there was now only a newspaper seller; and inside, where once there had been comfortable chairs and sofas on which to await one's friends, and a showcase or two displaying goods of quality, there was now nowhere to sit and only a small shop selling pennants, badges, mugs stamped with the Tower of London, toy guardsmen and beefeaters, and post-cards of the royal family. Beyond the massive reception desk, left over from handsomer times, a wide hallway carpeted with writhing patterns worn flat by innumerable feet led to a series of bars and restaurants, saccharined by Muzak and scented by generations of past meals.

Dave and Janice carried their bags into the lift and up to the fourth floor. Their room was a functional cell, with two icy-looking single beds, a tea-making machine, a television and a view on to a well from windows that did not open because of the air-conditioning.

They moved about somewhat awkwardly, bumping into each other in the narrow alleys between the furniture, and Dave gave her a big hug and a French kiss, bending her slightly towards one of the beds. But she was oddly nervous and evaded him — not strongly because if he wanted to have sex immediately then that was what he should have; but he smiled and let her go. He stretched out on the bed and watched while she changed and did her face, as if they were married, as if they had all the time in the world. They went downstairs to the Hi-Di-Ho bar for a drink, then into the Roastery for dinner, then out on the town.

That weekend was dreamlike for Janice. The

119

sequence of drink, food, film, music, the impersonal amenities of the bedroom, and, affectionate and good-humoured, Dave, kept her even more than usual in a haze of unreality. And when they finally got to bed, both of them a little blurred by drink and the echoes of the disco they had visited somewhere in the broken-down streets of Soho after the film, and he slid in beside her, naked as a fish, she was so bemused by it all that she was hardly conscious of what he was doing, too much distracted by the cold, crisp sheets and unfamiliar pillow, by the narrowness of the bed designed for only one and most of all by his nakedness — she had never experienced a naked man before. She was not even sure she liked it. When he murmured of her shortie nightdress (bought specially the day before), "Take it off," she refused quite violently. She was flustered by his warm slippery flesh, his out-crops of hair, his oily savoury smell — and her own, which surged out of their joint heat despite the aseptic freshness of the bed. In the darkness, in the flurry and flounder of the bedclothes, the slidings of his flesh on hers, she acquiesced, half in panic, half with a kind of despair — for she was in a foreign land, she could not understand and almost did not like the place where he was leading her. She should have reached that place but she did not; confusion held her back. She lay awake for quite a time after he had left her, listening to his breathing and musing on how unreal it was to be here in this impersonal room with a naked Dave. She almost wished for Grace, and fell asleep.

She awoke next morning when Dave got back into her bed. And this time she got there. It took her by surprise; and, like his nakedness, she was not sure she liked it. But reach it she must, in a great wrenching welter of terror and joy. And as she came out of it she was suffused with love; she clung and clasped as he urgently laboured above her, she would have killed him rather than let him go without wresting the same cataclysm from him too. He groaned, as she had screamed, and his collapsed weight on her brought triumph and subjugation beyond all knowledge: she would have died for him or killed him. He fell asleep.

When he awoke he was exceedingly cheerful, sang in the shower, slapped her bottom as he passed her, patted after-shave and combed his hair with attention. Left her to do her face and went downstairs to get a newspaper, would meet her in the lobby. She hurried, half-expecting he would not be there when she got down, vanished from her life and leaving her stranded as had so often been the case. Wham bam, thank you, ma'am — some didn't even stop to say thank you; all they wanted was a quick screw, but Dave, mysterious Dave, had wanted to get her as well as himself. Well, now he'd got her (she went weak and hot at the remembrance) so he would probably go too. Perhaps he would have paid the bill first, though she'd known some that wouldn't.

But he was there, reading the *Observer*, and took her elbow to lead her into the Snackery for breakfast. He ate the lot and persuaded her to fruit juice and scrambled eggs, although with Grace she never had more than a cup of tea. She began to feel hungry and strong and happy. She felt as though all her flesh were filling out, bouncy and smooth. She felt she wanted to touch him all the time, but he might not like that. She felt she would like to go back to the bedroom and do it all over again, but he didn't suggest that. He wanted to go out.

It was a fine morning and he made her walk along Piccadilly and into the park and up to Speakers' Corner. She had never known such a place existed. The park yes, she'd sometimes been in the park (mostly when she was skint and sort of on the game, before she met Grace) but this wide space with its good-humouredly jeering crowds and the people, black and white, standing up there on boxes or steps or whatever, shouting their heads off, making guys of themselves, hair and scarves and sometimes banners blowing in what seemed like gales of ridicule — she'd never seen anything like it. A pair of coppers stalked or stood on the outskirts, benign. The voices cracked and bellowed to and fro, needled by hecklers, wholly possessed by their fantasies, while beyond them the never-ending wall of traffic snorted around the Marble Arch and its springing fountains.

"Democracy in action," said Dave. He put his arm round her and squeezed her breast. She wished they could go straight back to the hotel but he moved her on to another group, still with his arm round her. "Pay attention. This is educational. This is what made our nation great."

"What is?"

He laughed and kissed her cheek. "Free speech, love."

"Eyey, on the job, I see!" A voice broke in behind them and they turned to see a thickset young man in an anorak regarding them quizzically. Dave released Janice.

"Hi, Porky. Small world."

"Getting smaller all the time." He looked from one to the other with a kind of indulgent menace. "Who's this, then?"

"Janice. This is Porky, a mate of mine."

"Hi, Janice."

"Hi."

He turned back to Dave, hands stuck into the pouches of his anorak in a curiously aggressive way. "You working?"

"No, weekend off. You?"

"Kind of. You never know."

"Yeah. Well. Be seeing you."

"Right on, boy." He grinned and watched them move away.

"Who was that?"

"A mate of mine," he repeated. He seemed put out and, taking her elbow, steered her away from the speakers and across Park Lane towards the Underground. "We'd best get back to the hotel, they want our bags out by twelve noon."

Back in the room, putting her bits and pieces into her tote bag, she'd looked at the still unmade beds longingly.

"I wish we could stay here for ever."

"If wishes were horses beggars would ride."

"What?"

"That's what my old grannie used to say."

"What did she mean?"

He zipped up his case, came and took her in his arms. "You're so bloody clueless, love, I sometimes wonder if you're real." His voice was teasing but his look and his touch were

124

tender. "Where've you been all your life, eh, you don't hardly know anything."

"Oh, Dave."

"Oh, Dave!" he mimicked, released her and patted her cheek. "Come on now, get your skates on. Whatsay we whiz down to Brighton for the rest of the day? I'll drop you back tonight, okay?"

Which they did.

She had told Grace she was going to an all-night party, which Grace accepted without a second thought. Janice had done it before and in fact Grace was quite glad to be on her own for a bit, to have a bit of a think.

She had given the Old George a miss the Sunday following her tea at Notting Hill Gate. However glad of an audience Mrs. Robinson might be, Robinson (Conroy!) was a wary bird and Grace was not going to seem too eager, too available.

He seemed pleased to see her two Sundays later, half-rising from his seat as usual as she approached, going to get her gin and vermouth with a nod and a queried "The usual?" She took off her head scarf and folded it neatly into her handbag, patting up the modest waves of her hair. The bar was its habitual murky self, with groups of jolly men and frisky women at every table and along the bar, where brighter lights made a stained-glass window of the ranked bottles. The Palm Court Musak oozed, unnoticed as air.

"*Votre santé,*" he said, raising his glass of wine.

"Cheers," she responded, taking a sip of her gin.

"Gave last Sunday a miss, did you?"

"I had a bit of a cold."

"Ah. Tricky, these summer colds."

"Yes."

A pause. Each of them sipped.

"My mother enjoyed your visit."

"That's nice. She's a grand old lady."

"I don't think of her as old."

"No, of course not. I just meant . . ."

"She was a bit of a beauty, you know. Well known."

"I'm sure."

"She left the stage when she married my father. Gave it all up. Tragic."

"But that radio serial . . ."

"She went back after my father died. He was a solicitor, left us comfortably off, of course, but Mother's not one to sit idle. She made her come-back in the Salt and Peppers — there's not many actresses with style like hers nowadays. She was a real *grande dame.*"

"I could see."

"And after that she went into the serial.

Right from the start, the original cast. She didn't regard it as real theatre, of course, but she never missed a recording."

"Fancy."

He refilled his glass, thereby emptying the bottle. He seemed to have come to the end of what he had to say and they sat in silence amid the impersonal hubbub of the bar, Grace carefully selecting her next remark.

"She still keeps in touch, I expect?"

"Well . . ." His heavy face grew fractionally heavier. "There's not many of them left now. And she can't get about."

"I wonder . . ." Grace paused, diffidence in the tilt of her head, the twist of her fingers round the stem of her glass. "Would she like me to pop in on her sometimes, have a bit of a chat? I don't want to intrude and I'm sure she's happy just to sit with her memories, but if you think she'd like me to visit her sometimes I'd be only too glad."

He seemed not quite as surprised as she had thought he would be, although his tone was warm. "That's very good of you. I'm sure you have many calls on your time."

"I could fit her in. It'd be a pleasure. I could just pop in for a cup of tea and a chat, do any bits of shopping or laundry perhaps, any little things like that. Once a week or so?"

"May I put it to her?"

"Do. I'd really enjoy it, someone like your mother. What stories she must have to tell! And I was a trained nurse, you know, so I'm quite to be trusted."

"I'm sure." He looked at her almost warmly. "It's very good of you. I'm sure she'd be pleased. She finds the days long with me at business all day."

"I expect she'll be glad when you retire. Anyone can see you're a wonderful son."

"She's a wonderful woman."

So it was agreed that he should sound his mother out and that if she liked the idea then he would leave a key with the porter every Wednesday afternoon (for even with her sticks it was an effort for Mrs. Robinson to get to the front door) and Grace would call and have a cup of tea with her. Grace was not keen on the porter; the fewer people that might ever recognise her the better, she had learned over the years. But it couldn't be helped, and in this case wouldn't matter since, however her plans turned out, everything would be open and above-board at least for a while. A Wednesday was quite convenient; she could work the nearby districts — Ladbroke Grove, Harrow Road, Shepherd's Bush — before dropping in on the old lady for a rest and reviving cup of tea.

They parted at the Underground, as usual,

with a modest but perceptible increase in warmth, each hopeful of the future. And the following Sunday when they met in the Old George, as usual, he told her his mother had agreed.

Grace approached this enterprise with the greatest care; it could perhaps be the most ambitious of her career. She considered whether she should take Mrs. Robinson a small gift of some kind, a pot plant or a half-pound box of chocolates but decided not to on this first occasion, it might be seen as "sucking up." This first visit must be dignified, the meeting of two mature ladies of which one was well aware of but not overawed by the once-eminence of the other, while the other could feel she was condescending but nevertheless grateful for an audience. For Grace's experience over the years in the homes and latterly on her own schemes had taught her that what old people wanted most was someone to talk at rather than to. Eighty or more years of life had filled them to over-flowing with themselves, there was no room left for anything else. And Grace knew she was perfectly well able to fend off with her polished carapace of lies any brief shafts of curiosity about herself that might from time to time occur.

They sat on either side of the gas fire, the light from a heavily fringed standard lamp bringing green tints into Mrs. Robinson's black hair. Someone had set a well-prepared tea tray on the table beside her chair and all Grace had to do was plug the electric kettle in beside the fireplace. Although the day was not cold the gas fire was burning and the room was hot, seeming hotter for the press of pictures of all kinds upon the walls, which were papered in rather shabby crimson with a satin stripe — 1950s style, Grace assessed. The furniture was unmatched and heavy and there was plenty of it; fringed brocade upholstery, rather worn on the arms, fringed or braided velvet and satin cushions, dark wooden tables with brocade runners on which stood framed photographs and a collection of china flowers of many varieties. It was a room as stuffed with Marion Conroy as Mrs. Robinson herself, and Grace wondered, as she drank her strong tea and declined the last scone (which Mrs. Robinson ate) how Conroy (Conroy!) could put up with it.

At first they spoke of nothing: the weather, the royal family, the price of things. From these Grace gleaned some facts: Mrs. Robinson never went out but if the weather were very good Conroy would settle her, well wrapped up, in the small walled patio beyond the curtains — hardly more than a yard, Mrs. Robinson declared, but it caught the sun and Conroy had some evergreens in tubs and a trellis with rambler roses up the back wall. And she could not be seen; privacy was so important, especially to those who knew what it was to be in the public eye. As she had. And, of course, the Queen.

They both agreed there was no one to equal the Queen, unless it were the Queen Mother. The younger royals were charming, slaves to duty no matter what the papers sometimes implied; there was an inbred Something, a distinction and dignity about them all which some people were born with. As she was.

Which meant, of course, that you didn't need to have a great deal of money in order to have good taste. Taste, style, just came naturally to some. There was little of either in the world today, especially in the arts. People and things were judged by what they cost not by what they were; Mrs. Robinson's domestic help, for instance, cost two pounds fifty an hour and did virtually nothing for it save mop over the kitchen and bathroom floors, Hoover the carpets and do such domestic shopping during the week as Conroy could not do. And she seldom bought the right brands and always the most expensive. As for the silver — if Conroy hadn't sat down and done it every fortnight it would have turned quite black!

So Grace filed away the facts, nodding and making sounds of agreement: they had a twice weekly charwoman and could afford her; Mrs. Robinson was housebound but healthy; and Conroy was more of a puzzle than she had thought, domesticated and docile yet, at the Old George, stubbornly his own man.

She left well before he was due home from business. At this stage, one of them at a time was enough.

She went again the following Wednesday (after a useful morning around the Harrow Road where, despite the conurbations of council blocks, she found a few enclaves of old terraces in the basements of which still nested some likely old dears for the next day). This time she brought a bunch of carnations and was sent into the kitchen to find a vase. In a quick survey she saw tidiness and dirty corners, the mark of male domesticity and scamped charring; some good silver; a full store-cupboard with the accent on roughage; and a wine rack stacked with claret as well as two unopened bottles of Johnny Walker — she had noted an open bottle and glasses on a side table in the lounge. Nothing on the kitchen walls save an electric clock and a calendar illustrated with pictures of historic houses.

"How good of you," said Mrs. Robinson when Grace brought the filled vase back. "I do so enjoy fresh flowers. I remember the wonderful bouquets one used to get on first night — brought on from the wings by the house manager, you know, quite overwhelming. To make one's curtsy — I *never* bowed — with an armful of flowers called for all one's training in deportment. Not that I was ever frail you know — it just came naturally. Some actresses have it — Mrs. Pat, for instance, Gladys Cooper never. She never played Shakespeare."

The electric kettle began to steam and Grace was allowed to make the tea.

Apropos of apparently nothing, the old lady suddenly asked, "Do you drink, Mrs. Black?"

Care was needed in her answer, in view of the whisky bottle on the side table. She smiled. "Well — just the occasional nip."

"You met Conroy in a public house."

"That's right, the Old George near Oxford Street. It's more of a club really, you see the same people there week after week, a nice class of person."

Mrs. Robinson set down her cup with a sour look on her large face. "Conroy insists on his Sunday evenings there. I tell him I'm alone all the week and the weekends should be the family time. But no. He says he likes the company."

"It's the same for me — it's the company."

"But there's no one special? What company is he in?"

"Well, none really, no one special. Like I said, it's the same for me. It's nice to get out and just be among a cheery crowd. You don't need to mix with them, just be among them. I used to go with my niece Janice, I expect I told you. She liked a bit of a crowd at the weekend, working all week and a quiet sort of girl, not one to be gadding about on her own. Me and her used to like sitting there quietly, watching the world go by and listening to the music. Sometimes we'd get talking, like your son and me did, but not often."

"You've a niece?"

"Yes, my sister's girl. I've taken care of her ever since my sister passed away — oh, twelve, fifteen years ago. She's a sweet girl, a social worker. We're just like sisters really, despite the generation gap — you find that sometimes, don't you, age doesn't seem to matter, you can be real pals. But she's got this boyfriend now, see, so I have to go on my own." She smiled wryly and finished her tea.

Mrs. Robinson's thoughts veered away. "That's how it is nowadays. Young people only think of themselves. I suppose it's different if you've grown up with the team spirit. I mean, in the theatre you're all one splendid family together for as long as the run of the play, all good troopers together. I remember when I first joined the BBC Rep . . ." She was off.

Grace did not go to the Old George that Sunday. Let him and his mother simmer together a little.

"Are you a theatre-goer, Mrs. Black?" the old lady asked the following Wednesday. She had permitted Grace to buy for her on the way to the flat a jar of moisturising face cream and a small tin of laxative pills — "personal things I don't quite like to ask my woman to buy." Repayment had been strictly made, and Grace knew that Mrs. Robinson was now aware that Grace was useful. She was allowed the freedom of the kitchen and, in the natural course of things, the bathroom — very dank and dark, looking out on to a wall, with grips round the bath and lavatory seat to help Mrs. Robinson up and down, a non-slip mat in the bath itself, a great many bath oils and talcums, laxatives, analgesics, cough medicines in one side of the cupboard over the basin, in the other shaving cream, razor, several preparations for dental care, indigestion tablets and a large jar of multivitamin pills. She had managed a peep into the large front bedroom and did not need more; she already knew as much as was necessary about Mrs. Robinson. The small bedroom was more difficult to glimpse, for the door was always shut and there was no reason whatever for her to open it. She was almost tempted to slip one of her professional powders into the old girl's tea as she made it so as to have time for a good old look, but that was too risky. It was, after all, a test of Grace's ingenuity either to penetrate Conroy's bedroom and the information it must hold or exact such information from his mother.

To Mrs. Robinson's question she responded cautiously, "Well, I'm afraid not really, no."

"Americans have such a high opinion of the London theatre. I remember friends from over the herring-pond having such admiration for our productions and of course now, I believe, for our television. It's a pity that radio doesn't export — although I believe that even over there they had heard of 'Nanny Jane's Journal.' "

"I used to listen to that, it was ever so popular. We all knew Lady Belhampton."

Mrs. Robinson acknowledged the tribute with a small smile. "Who were 'we,' as a matter of interest?"

"The patients — and staff, of course, if we

were off duty. I'm a trained nurse, you know."

"Conroy did mention it. Where did you train?"

"In the Midlands — St. Michael's in Wolverhampton." She had learned long ago that the Robinsons were southerners, come in his childhood from Guildford.

"You were there in the war? Or were you too young?"

Grace laughed deprecatingly. "You're having me on! I was in the forces during the war. I went straight from school into the ATS, green as a gooseberry I was. And then I found myself up in Scotland somewhere doing Intelligence. Codes and that."

"Codes. As at Bletchley?"

"It was several places and ever so secret. Even now I wouldn't like to say just where we were." Which she reckoned took care of that.

"Of course," said Mrs. Robinson after a pause, "there were splendid ENSA companies during the war. I toured in *The School for Scandal*, Lady Sneerwell. I wonder you didn't choose nursing straightaway for your wartime service?"

"I didn't know my own mind, you know what young girls are."

"And when did you meet your husband?"

Harry, slipping his hand up her skirt behind the Naafi counter. "At St. Michael's. We were training together."

"A doctor?"

"No — he went into dispensing, prescriptions and that." Far safer. Better attack. "Your husband must have missed you while you were touring round like that."

"He had already died. He was never robust and many years older than I. I gave up the stage when I married, you know, but after his death and with Britain at war I felt I had to return to do my bit. ENSA was a tremendous experience, quite tremendous. The team spirit in excelsis. Travelling here and there, coaches, lorries, playing in camps and hangars to all those dear boys — I shall never forget it. Such wonderful audiences!"

"Your little boy must have missed his mummy."

"He was sixteen and at boarding-school. And where did you and your husband settle, once you were qualified?"

"Oh, we stayed in the Midlands. I only came south after he passed away, I took up private nursing." You never knew where old people might have been in hospital one time or another. Although this one looked tough as an old boot. "Have you lived in this flat long, you and your son?"

"Oh yes, a very long time. I was making my comeback then, the first of the Salt and Pepper comedies, and my poor boy was off doing his national service. He knew he always had a home here with me."

"And you've been together ever since? I think that's lovely."

"Well no, not quite all the time. He was away for a period. Would you be good enough to pass me the *Radio Times* — I believe an old friend of mine is in the police series this evening." Grace complied, then began stacking the tea things on to the tray. That would do for today. She was not dissatisfied with what she had learned and had given out only misinformation in return. She would have to find out what it was that had separated him from this boring old cow and why he had rejoined her, but not today.

Mrs. Robinson watched her, her eyes sharp between their brightly blued lids that accentuated the pouches above the rouged cheeks. She asked abruptly, "You never considered marrying again?"

Grace laughed. "Bless you, no! I'd not give up my independence for anyone, not at my age. Besides, there was no one quite like my Harry." You could say that again!

She picked up the tray and took it into the kitchen. As she washed up the tea things and put them away she congratulated herself on having got in that important statement so early on, and not at her own initiative. For it was absolutely essential the old dear shouldn't think that Grace was after her Conroy.

"My mother wonders if you'd care to take supper with us on Sunday next," said Conroy heavily, turning the wineglass by its stem and gazing out towards the Space Invaders churning and clicking above the Muzak.

"That's very kind of her." Her response was reserved. "I don't want to put you to any trouble."

"You won't," he said, and sank into silence. He seemed glum.

She understood why when she arrived at their flat the following Sunday. The table in the french windows looking out on to the yard was nicely laid and Mrs. Robinson came to it with the aid of her sticks, shaking off Grace's hand at her elbow. Conroy brought in and served the food, which he had cooked; a green soup with a dollop of cream in it which Grace didn't care for; roast lamb tasting a bit peculiar and with tiny bits of some sort of twig in it which got between her teeth; crisp roast potatoes and slightly raw runner beans; ice cream with some sort of fruity sauce over it. There was a bottle of red wine of which Conroy drank most, as he had brought his mother's pre-supper whisky glass to the table for her.

"Wherever did you learn to cook?" cried Grace.

"Here and there."

"Conroy can turn his hand to anything," said Mrs. Robinson.

"It was a case of needs must," he said, and refilled his glass.

After dinner he brought in a tray of tiny cups and very strong coffee; Grace was dying for a cup of tea, for the wine had made her thirsty and the coffee made it worse. Conroy refused to let her help with the washing-up, which his mother said he would do later. She was recounting again her early days at the Memorial Theatre at Stratford-upon-Avon before the war and her marriage, and not much response was called for from either Grace or her son. They watched the nine o'clock news and then Grace said she must be getting home.

"Conroy will walk you to the station," said his mother.

It was a fine night, stars and a sharp moon sailing high in a sky dark enough to reflect the sultry glare of London. They turned into the narrow hill of Church Street, almost empty at this dead pause of the evening, the occasional bus riding by like a huge bright box, the windows of the closed antique shops giving out only the muted sparkle of a chandelier, the milky glow of china. As they neared Notting Hill Gate itself there were more people, brighter lights from the restaurants where waiters idled beside the displayed antipasti, waiting for the customers who would come when cinemas and West End theatres closed.

"That was ever such a lovely meal," Grace said. "It was a real treat. Wherever did you learn?"

"I've always liked cooking." Which was no answer.

"Well, it was certainly an eye-opener to me and no mistake."

He seemed pleased. "Yes, well. I don't do that sort of dinner often. Mother's not got many friends left and besides, to be frank" — he paused but decided to continue, his big face above his big body expressionless as ever — "I rather treasure my evenings up West."

Grace murmured something suitable.

"She's a wonderful woman," he continued, taking her elbow to cross a side street and immediately releasing it, "and of course she's alone all day most of the time, with me at business. But I've always maintained that I must have time to myself once or twice a week.

She's come to accept that but it wasn't easy. She's a woman of very strong will."

"I can see that."

"She's taken to you. I hoped she would."

"That's nice." They had reached the Bayswater Road and turned into the wide brightly lit street towards the steps down into the Underground.

"It's a matter of principle for me, you understand," he said. "It's right and proper that I should look after Mother now she can't get about, but everyone needs a bit of independence. That's my opinion."

"That's right."

"She's a wonderful woman, wonderful. She had a great career, you know, everyone in the theatre world knew her. But that's years ago. Naturally she feels lonely now."

"How long have you been together?" she ventured.

"Eight, nine years."

"So you were off on your own a long time before that." She made it a statement rather than a question, which she sensed would not be answered, but even so all he said was "Yes." Like drawing teeth, she thought sourly, holding out her hand with a genteel smile at the top of the Underground steps.

"Well," she said, "thanks ever so much for a really nice evening."

He took her hand and held it a moment. "It's been a pleasure. Shall you be at the Old George next Sunday?"

"I daresay. We both need our nights off, don't we?"

"Yes." His large pink face (so like his mother's) softened into an almost mischievous smile. "Playing hookey, eh?"

"That's right." They smiled together. "Well, *au revoir* then."

"*Au revoir.*"

She turned away and went down the steps, opening her hand-bag to find her senior citizen's travel pass. All the way home she sorted out what she had learned; it was not very much but enough to build on.

5

Grace had a lot on her mind these days. Apart from her preoccupations with the Robinsons there was still the day-to-day chore of earning a living for Janice and herself: the selection of an area not previously worked (not too near one that had), the disposal of the proceeds. Added to which an exceptionally wet few weeks had made her reconnaissances unpleasant with constantly damp feet and soaked umbrella, and had kept many of the old folk indoors more often than not so that they were hard to find and follow. It was really hard work, and more and more she realised that it was time for a change.

What with so much to think about she had hardly noticed what Janice was like these days. They still, of course, lived side by side, slept in the same bed, cooked snacks in the screened kitchenette in the corner of the living room. Janice still took their washing to the launderette, did their shopping, signed on for her supplementary every fortnight, renewed her sleeping-pills prescription every month. They both often listened to the programmes on the good Roberts radio they had picked up on one of their earlier jobs; it had been heavy to carry away but not too big for Janice's tote bag. Grace liked "Baker's Dozen."

She had barely noticed that beneath Janice's customary dreaminess there had lately been a sort of excitement, a sense that she was hugging a happy secret. Her face seemed fuller, her complexion was better, and her hair no longer hung in lank curtains but, with the aid of body-giving gels and Carmen rollers, swung in a way which minimised her long nose and jaw. Her figure had always been good and now she moved as though she were aware of it, enjoyed being inside it. Grace, if she noticed any change at all, assumed it was because Janice had got in with a congenial crowd somewhere. What Janice did in her own time had never been any concern of Grace's; so long as she did her job properly, as she had done since she had been reprimanded, Grace was not bothered. Janice was simply part of the set-up, a tool that worked to Grace's design, to be taken up or put down as Grace decided.

So Grace was extremely put out when

Janice, winding a lock of hair nervously round her finger one Tuesday morning just as Grace was getting ready to go out, said, "Grace — I'll be working this Saturday."

Grace stood still. "You what?"

"I'll be working. I got a Saturday job, round at the supermarket in Keatings Road." In Grace's silence she hurried on, "It's only Saturdays, it won't interfere none with you and me, I was definite about that. It's just Saturdays, ten till seven, helping in the shop and that."

"That Greek shop?"

"That's right. It's all family, see, but his daughter's having a baby and he wants someone to help out for a week or two, and it's all cash, no insurance nor anything, just helping out."

Grace clicked shut her handbag and sat down slowly by the table. Janice was still in her dressing-gown and stood apprehensively watching Grace's expressionless face.

"Why?" Grace asked coldly.

Janice looked away, the hair twirling round her finger. "I just thought it'd be nice to have a bit of my own. You know, like pin money. It won't interfere with you and me. It's only Saturdays."

"We sell Saturdays."

"Well, you do most of it, always have."

147

"Now I'll have to do it all, won't I?"

"Yes, well, you do it better than me anyway."

"That's true enough." She sat for a moment in silence. "I don't like it."

"Well, it's done!"

"Once you get working regular you never know where it'll end."

"I told you, it's all in cash!"

"And supposing someone from the Labour pops in for a pot of yoghurt? What you going to do then?"

"They won't! And even if they did I could say I was just helping out, couldn't I? It's not like I was there every day."

"You should have asked me, Janice," she said, getting to her feet again and knotting the scarf at her neck. It was a bright day for once, but she'd take an umbrella.

"It's only Saturdays," Janice repeated.

"It had better be," said Grace, and left the house. She was quite thrown.

Since teaming up with Grace, Janice had never shown any desire whatever to get a regular job, content to drift along under Grace's direction, as passive as a fish in a tank. Why now had she suddenly shown this burst of independence, and without letting on to Grace first?

The reason, unknown to Grace, was Dave. When Janice had stopped accompanying her to the Old George of a Sunday Grace had simply assumed that she had fallen in with some crowd with a regular meeting-place, a disco or a club or something of that sort, and was certainly not interested enough to ask.

She could not know that Janice, suffused by the revelations that Dave's body had brought her, was eager now to please him in every way she could. And as their relationship grew more tender he had begun to tease her more, press her a little: "I don't know how you fill your days, I don't really." "I reckon you'll fall asleep one day and wake up a hundred years later." "When you going to realise your potential, you dozy wally?" All of it gentle, not (to be honest) all that much bothered, simply as if it puzzled and mildly saddened him that she was content to pass her life in what must seem total idleness.

Well, filling the shelves and stacking the wire baskets for Mr. Theodore on Saturdays wasn't much but it was a start. She could maybe go on to working Mondays and Tuesdays too (days Grace never wanted her), might even take over the till. If she could learn which buttons to push. And not be tempted — Greeks were sharp as needles. Mr. Theodore would pay her in cash as long as she wanted, for it suited him as well as it suited her, no problem. The only problem was Grace, who could turn quite nasty if you didn't do just as she wanted.

But if Janice had a job, then Dave would be pleased. And if he were pleased he would think more of her and then the two of them might, he might suggest . . . And then Janice wouldn't need Grace.

"You what?" Dave echoed Grace when Janice told him. They were kissing in his car up near the Whitestone pond in Hampstead as usual, the dark trees of the heath falling away below them to the orange glow of Golders Green, Wembley, Harrow in the distance, counterpaned by a sky of heavy clouds from which rain misted down. July! The car heater was on and Janice longed to move into the back but Dave hadn't suggested it. He was not always all that keen, not like most she'd been in cars with; he had to be in the mood, which made it all the more wonderful when he was. He had never suggested repeating that dreamlike weekend in the hotel; sometimes that seemed like a fantasy to her now, but his skills with her body, even in the awkward back of the car, assured her it was not. She would never forget it, never; and even when she sometimes did not quite reach that same wild place, he brought her instead a peace and tenderness she was too timid to call love. He made it something special, even in the back of the car.

"I've got a job. In a shop. I'm the cashier."

"You're kidding."

"No, honest."

"You can't add two beans together!"

She pulled away. She had her pride still — sometimes. "Yes I can. Anyway it's all a machine."

"What sort of shop?"

"A supermarket. Continental."

"Well I'm buggered!"

"I thought you'd be pleased."

"I am, love, I am." He pulled her close again but she knew he was laughing.

"I don't see what's so funny."

"It's just I never thought you'd join the workers. Not with your bad back."

"It's better these days," she said sulkily. She often forgot she was supposed to have it still, although every month she called at the surgery with her renewal of prescription form for Grace.

"Whatever made you do it? Benefits getting dodgy?"

She pulled away again, really cross now. "Leave off!"

"I mean it."

"I thought you'd be pleased," she repeated. "You're always getting at me."

"Never!"

"Yes you are. Saying I'm useless, nothing to do all day and that."

"I was joking."

"No you weren't, you're always getting at me. Well, I'm not useless, I can get a job like anyone else. I just walked in and asked him and he jumped at me."

"Aye-aye!"

"Not that sort of jump! I'm serious. You never treat me serious."

He pulled her close again and kissed her, his hand on her breast. "I always treat you serious."

"No you don't," but feeling his hand and the tremors it woke in her, her thoughts slid to the back seat.

"You mean you're a sex object?" he murmured.

"Am I? Oh, Dave . . ."

Twenty minutes later, back in the front seats again, with a tape playing, he said after a while, "You're a good girl, Jan. You're daft but you're a good girl."

"You do — fancy me?"

"Yeah, I fancy you. God knows why, for you're a real wally. Daft as a baby, you are. You must appeal to the mother in me."

She stirred. "You're always joking!"

"So that I may not cry. Never mind." He kissed her cheek, removed his arm from her shoulders, switched on the car lights. "Fact is I'm stuck with you for a while, Jan. Don't ask me why. Maybe it's just because you're so bloody helpless."

He started the engine.

She was still too well trained by Grace to have let him know exactly where she lived, and he dropped her at the corner of the High Street as usual. There she kissed him long and meltingly, putting into it all the subservient love he had brought into her life and which she had neither the words nor the awareness to express. He stroked her hair, his eyes almost rueful, still amused. "Seeya," he said. She got out of the car and stood to watch him drive away. She would have died for him.

Fantasies filled her days: him and her on holiday in the Caribbean, on a cruise, stretched out in the sun in Benidorm. Or, best of all, just living together — in a room, in a flat, a big double bed and a duvet like she saw in the magazines and a wardrobe with her clothes on one side and his on the other; and a nice little kitchen, all modern, where she'd cook for him — she'd buy books and learn how. And a lounge with stereo and a video and a big white leather settee. Or just

153

his flat where he lived now and never let her come to. Why not? Why wouldn't he? Was it really his landlady? Who had that man been they'd talked to at Speakers' Corner? He never said, only that they were mates. Where?

Sometimes just for a moment, she wondered if Dave could be — well, dodgy? Running something, like she and Grace were. A robber, even, cool? But no, he was too clean, too easy — wasn't he? Why did she know so little about him when he knew all about her? True, it was mostly lies, but she'd told him, hadn't she? He'd told her nothing, not really, and now she was afraid to press in case he got annoyed and dropped her.

She let it go. She had long learned to be content with what she got. But when would they ever be in a bed together, all night, shockingly naked, stormed and transformed . . . ?

She thought about him all the time, whether at home with Grace in their bed-sit and kitchenette or stocking the shelves at Continental Delicacies or making the tea with her back turned to some old woman while Grace, her documents imposingly spread out, stunned the old thing with double talk.

"Did you put the sugar in, Mary?" Grace had to say sharply. The old thing, sunk like a toad in a sagging armchair, said, "I don't take sugar."

"You ought to take sugar, dear," said Grace, "it gives you energy," and gave Janice a nod to put in an extra pinch of the pills.

For Grace had to watch Janice all the time now when they were on a job. God knows what had got into the girl. They had even at one point run short of pills because Janice had forgotten to get her prescription.

"What're you thinking of, gel?" Grace had cried, for once raising her voice, "How d'you think we can operate without no bloody pills?"

"I forgot," Janice said sulkily, "My back's not been bothering me."

"Your back! Your back's not been bothering you since you come out of Holloway but that don't mean we don't need the pills, you silly cow! With all your hard work at the super-market, bending and carrying cartons and that," she added sarcastically, "I'd've thought you needed them worse than ever."

"I can't let on I'm working."

"You don't have to let on anything, you just get a repeat for your bloody pills!" It was unlike Grace to use strong language but really, Janice was too much! The time had definitely come for a change.

The Robinsons were coming along nicely. Her Wednesday visits were established; wher-ever she had been hunting her old folk she now always ended up in Notting Hill at three-thirty, got the key from the porter, with whom she had become on ladylike good terms, let herself in with a cheery "Cooee, it's me" and spent the next couple of hours keeping Mrs. Robinson happy. Mostly this consisted of listening to her talking about herself and her career, going through the musty pages of her cuttings books, or sometimes admiring the stage jewellery still kept in old chocolates boxes or the half-dozen resplendent costumes, smelling of the greasepaint that marked their edges, that hung in her wardrobe, cloaked in plastic. But she also gave the old lady manicures, cut her toenails, did personal shopping such as rouge and Steradent, and served dainty teas, for which she usually brought in, at her own expense, the miniature Danish pastries the old girl wolfed.

She was careful not to seem to pry, but having the run of the kitchen and Mrs. Robinson's bedroom (a dark room full of furniture, smelling of camphor and scent) had been able to pick up a good deal of information. A fur stole (squirrel, not worth much) and a Persian lamb coat (worth a good deal more) hung in plastic bags in the mahogany wardrobe, never worn now as neither were the velvet and silk dresses, the high-heeled shoes lined up below. In a leather case (the all too obvious place) was a collection of not negligible jewellery — garnets, pearls, a large aquamarine ring, fat Edwardian bracelets. The dressing-table was a clutter of cosmetics and a full set of embossed silver brushes, not well cleaned. On the mantelpiece was a photograph of a startled-looking man, high-collared and bald-headed — the husband presumably; and a larger picture of Mrs. Robinson herself swathed in satin and with bobbed hair, holding on her lap a quite handsome child. Mrs. Robinson's expression was of smiling tenderness, her head and arms bent protectively round the boy, whose face was calm. Conroy, of course.

Grace could linger in this bedroom, since she was there at Mrs. Robinson's request. With Conroy's room she could only nip in and out surreptitiously, and learned little. It was smaller than his mother's, and bare. There were no photographs of any kind and the only pictures on the wall were engravings of Windsor and Edinburgh castles.

What did interest Grace was the existence of a small room next to the front door. Although used as a box-room, storing luggage and a card table, the Hoover, stacked pictures, spare blankets, it was a vestigial bedroom, with divan, chest of drawers, cupboard. Cleared, it would do very well for a housekeeper.

She never saw Conroy on her visits to the

flat; she had gone by the time he returned from business. But their Sunday meetings at the Old George continued. Since getting to know both him and his mother, Grace had come to realise that Conroy was immovable where his own wishes were concerned. On the face of it he was the attentive son to a domineering mother; but no matter how much Mrs. Robinson might hint or tease or complain he would not budge one inch from his small areas of independence. Sunday evenings were one. "Mother understands we each need a bit of a breather," he said stolidly when once Grace delicately probed. And when, on another occasion, she had said, almost idly, "I wonder you don't run a car, just for the convenience," he had replied, "I did have one a few years back, but Mother liked me to take her out for a run every weekend and that wasn't always convenient." He had said no more and Grace could for the moment think of no comment. The flat implacability of his response gave her something to think about.

Once, when Mrs. Robinson was rambling on about her hardships running a career and bringing up a son, Grace ventured, "He never married, then, a handsome boy like that?"

Mrs. Robinson's face had grown as stony as her son's could be. "Marriage doesn't suit everyone."

Grace knew better than to continue. Perhaps he was gay after all, some of those big heavy masculine types were the worst. But she didn't think he was; he was probably just one of those men who didn't need sex. There were more of them than you'd think.

Once Grace decided something she always acted quickly. The following Wednesday, having given Mrs. Robinson a half-pound of Black Magic chocolates and her tea, she excused herself "to spend a penny" and shut herself in the bathroom. Here she liberally rubbed the area between door and lavatory pan with moistened soap; it came up in a nice high gloss and even her sensible shoes found it slippery. She then pulled the plug and rejoined Mrs. Robinson for a half-hour or so's listen before making moves to leave.

"Well, I must love you and leave you," she said, plumping up the cushions against which she had leaned. "I've left everything nice and tidy in the kitchen and I'll see you again next week. Touch wood." She began putting on her cardigan, which had lain over the back of her chair. "D'you think you should go to the toilet while I'm still here? Then you'll be all nice and settled till your son gets home."

"Well, perhaps . . ." Mrs. Robinson began to heave herself forward, a coy expression on her face. "There's a rather naughty saying I

159

used to hear — Never refuse a pumpship. Among men, of course."

Grace passed her walking-sticks to her and gave a hand as the old lady hauled herself up, steadied and got her balance. Standing up she was not nearly so big as she was while sitting in her chair, but instead a stout, short figure with bowed shoulders, her large head with its jetty hair overweighting her body. She began to move towards the door, Grace hovering beside her into the passage. There Grace left her and went into the kitchen, rattling about and keeping a sharp ear. She heard the clump-clump of the footsteps along the carpet, the bathroom door opening, three more clump-clumps, a slither, a shriek, a crash.

She rushed towards the bathroom.

Mrs. Robinson lay on the floor, one walking-stick still in her hand, the second skidded towards the bath. She lay on her back but her limbs were at normal angles although a shoe had come off. Her face was purple but as Grace arrived it went completely grey, save for the scarlet and black of lipstick and eyebrows.

"Whatever have you done!" cried Grace.

Then followed a period of great activity. Grace's time in the old people's homes proved useful indeed as she was able to lug Mrs.

160

Robinson up, get her undressed and into bed, give her sweet tea, hot-water bottles and aspirin. She examined her arms and legs but found no fractures, only bruises already beginning to surface on the swollen, blue-veined pillows of her legs. "My word, you'll be like a rainbow tomorrow!"

Mrs. Robinson was uncharacteristically quiet during all this. Her colour had more or less returned but her breathing was loud and she was passive under Grace's attention, content to lie back on the pillows and sip the tea that Grace held to her lips. Shock took them like this, Grace knew; and realised too that Mrs. Robinson knew that the shock of her fall had caused her to wet herself, a humiliation worth a lot to Grace. It also required Grace to wash the bathroom floor, so that no trace of slipperiness remained.

"Shall I telephone your son?" she asked as, the tea and aspirin taken, Mrs. Robinson closed her eyes.

Grace noted that his number was that of the head office, and was put straight through. "Nothing to worry about," she said, after explaining what had happened, "but at her age, of course, it's shaken her up. I'll hang on here till you get back."

"It's very good of you," he said heavily an hour or so later. Mrs. Robinson was asleep

161

and they stood in the hall as Grace got ready to leave.

"I'm only thankful I was here. She'd have been lying there helpless else and we don't want pneumonia, do we."

He had suggested calling the doctor but Grace had said wait and see how she was in the morning. "There's nothing broken, that I do know, and we don't want to alarm her. A good night's sleep and I think she'll be as right as rain, once the shock's over. But I'd keep her in bed for a day or two, just to be on the safe side."

"Yes." He considered sombrely. "It's very awkward."

"Can you get in touch with your weekly woman, ask her to pop in for an extra hour or two?"

"I don't know her address."

"Oh dear, that *is* awkward. I don't think she ought to be left on her own all day, not for a day or two anyway." She put a scarf over her head and knotted it under her chin. "I wish I could help out myself but I've got commitments the next two days, right the other side of London. I do voluntary social work, see, visiting and that, and I can't let my old folk down, much as I'd like to help out. You could try getting a district nurse."

"No, she wouldn't like that. I've tried that before."

"Still . . ." She considered, buttoning her jacket. "It's not really right, is it? I mean, you being a man and all. And having to stay off business, I daresay you've got all kinds of important meetings and things." He nodded glumly. "I tell you what — I'll pop over Sunday, shall I, and give you a hand? You leave all her washing and toilet and that and I'll pop over Sunday dinnertime and get you all straightened out. Give you a break, too. How would that be?"

"I don't want to impose . . ."

"Get away! I only wish I could help tide over the next few days — but I can't let my old folk down, can I, not without warning. I'll pop over Sunday, around twelve."

They were at the front door, which she opened, letting in a waft of dank air from the outside corridor.

He loomed over her. "I'm more grateful than I can say . . ."

"Nonsense. If we can't all help each other in time of trouble . . . Keep her in bed, though, it's a shock at her age. And send for the doctor if you think there's the least need. I expect he'll say that, wonderful though she is, she didn't really ought to be left on her own all day, not at her age and being disabled. But

163

what can you do? Life has to go on, doesn't it. Well, I'll say good night and don't you worry. You get a good night's sleep. I'll be over Sunday."

She had Janice out and at work with her before eleven next morning, for once she had embarked on a scheme she liked to move fast. She had three subjects marked down for today, and she knew from experience that the best time to catch them was after they had laboriously concluded their rising and dressing but before they toddled out to the shops; or else, better still, tea-time, when they were hardly awake from their afternoon nap. All three were in the Kentish Town area for, with the knowledge that she would soon be done with all this, Grace no longer bothered about working far from her own base.

So they moved briskly about the small grey streets to the houses Grace had marked down on the previous days — Mrs. Black with her large briefcase full of documents, Mary with the tote bag big enough to engulf all sorts of things.

The first old lady was so deaf Grace was almost afraid the neighbours would hear the conversation through the party wall; but of course they were all of them out at work or about their business of whatever kind, and the spiel and the documents and the cups of tea all went down perfectly. There weren't many pickings there but the old thing hadn't spent any of her pension yet, and there was quite a bit tucked into a shortbread tin pushed under the bed with a pair of slippers, a chamberpot and a lot of fluff.

They had a snack in the High Street and went on to the next, a little old spinster, small and light as the husk of an insect, meticulously neat though with poor eyesight. They drank tea from fine china cups as she told them that she did voluntary work two mornings a week preparing dressings at the nearby hospital, where for many years she had been the first female physiotherapist they had ever employed and where she still felt "one of the team." Educated and intelligent as she was, she was fairly soon no match for Grace's rigmarole, although she asked some sharp questions to begin with. She went out like a light — much faster than most of them; and had some very nice things indeed, as well as a nice bit of cash.

The last one was a dead loss: door on the chain and apparently quite unable to speak or understand English. Not an Asian (Grace never did Asians), a European of some kind, but agitated and incomprehensible through the few open inches of the door. Grace didn't waste time; if you can't get in quick, get out quick was her maxim. Janice's tote bag was already full enough, and they returned home satisfied. Grace divided the cash and sold the articles as usual on the following Saturday. Janice did her Saturday at the supermarket, washed her hair, and then on Sunday went out for the day and most of the night, leaving Grace free.

As usual, Grace was absent for most of the following Monday and Tuesday. On Wednesday Janice returned from an early drink and a McDonald's with Dave before he went on late shift, to find most of Grace's belongings gone and a note on the dressing-table under a bottle of nail varnish:

Dear Jan,
Sorry to leave without saying cheerio but something come up too good to miss. Rent paid up to end of month and have left some 10ps (gas meter) in saucer in case you run out. All the best —

Grace

Part Two

6

Detective Inspector "Wally" Simpson banged
the knocker of the front door of 12 Malplaquet
Road, one of a terrace of two-storey red brick
villas with cream trim built at the turn of the
century and standing up pretty well to the
decline of prosperity and the traffic that passed
them as a through route to Camden Town.
The small front garden of number 12 had been
concreted over and its privet hedge cut down,
rather inexpertly, to waist height. Dustbins
clustered neatly in a corner and the whole
place was well kept though shabby; paint on
the window-frames and the door was cracking
at the seams, but the coloured glass panels in
the front door were clean. There was a bell
with names on yellowing bits of card stuck
on the bricks beside it, with instructions as
to how many times to ring for each, but Simpson knew there was no point in ringing that
marked "Frimwell"; so he banged the knocker
and waited while his sergeant, Terry "Wogan"
Blane, stared sternly around. Blane was keen.

"Good morning, sir. CID here." He showed his identification card with a winning smile. "I wonder if we might have a word?"

"Come in." The old man was small, bent and bald but taut and brown as a nut. They followed him down a dark uncluttered passage to the back room, once a kitchen, now an office-library in a corner of which was crammed a rug-covered divan.

"Please." The old man gestured towards it and an armchair by the unlit gas fire. He himself sat down at the desk, which was neatly piled with papers and open reference books. Such walls as did not have bookshelves along them were hung closely with prints and photographs, the prints of medieval-looking castles and landscapes, the photographs more modern — army groups and several of a middle-aged woman. Over the fireplace hung a Sacred Heart with a small votive lamp, flanked by saints and a large picture of the Pope.

Simpson and Blane seated themselves primly side by side on the divan. Simpson was a nice-looking man in his early thirties, in casual clothes and with an easy manner; Blane much younger, pink and white and stiff as an iced cake. He took out his notebook as Simpson asked, "Mr. Stanislas Sobieski?"

"I have that honour."

"A distinguished name, sir."

"You are aware?" The old man beamed.

"My dad was at Cassino. He read a bit afterwards, the history and that. Some of it rubbed off on me."

"Not a direct descendant, I fear. Probably not a descendant at all. But a good name to bear."

"Indeed." A little pause hung. "It's about Miss Frimwell, sir."

"I guessed as much."

"You're the landlord?"

"I am. After the war I used my gratuity to buy this then not very expensive property. My wife, an English lady I met about that time, arranged it all for lodgers. She is deceased now, some six years. But I learned from her and my lodgers are good."

"Miss Frimwell . . . ?"

"For many years, soon after my wife's death. She was a most charming gentlewoman."

"Perhaps you'd just tell us, sir, the sequence of events as you saw them. We have the facts, of course, but a firsthand account would be helpful."

Mr. Sobieski was silent for a moment, looking at the two policemen speculatively. Simpson looked blandly back, while Blane studied the room as though each object in it was suspect.

"This is a very quiet house. None of my

171

lodgers is young. This means we don't see much of each other, we keep ourselves to ourselves, as the English saying is. There is a bathroom on each floor — my wife's idea, unusual at the time — but shared to a strict timetable. Each room has its own kitchenette. Because I am the landlord I have allowed myself more space . . ." He gestured to the second door in the room, cloaked behind a velour curtain. "Out there is my kitchen, in here nothing but books. When my wife was living we had the front room also. Afterwards, Miss Frimwell."

"She was fit and well, sir, was she? Able to look after herself?"

"Entirely so. She was frail, of course, because she was not young. I don't know exactly . . ."

"She was eighty-five, sir."

"So. She was still working, you know."

"Yes, sir, two mornings a week. But not on the day of her decease."

Mr. Sobieski smiled sadly. "I was not aware even of that. I never knew which days she was in or out, so complete is our respected privacy."

Simpson allowed a pause before prompting. "The events of the seventh, sir?"

"Yes." He collected himself. "A Saturday. There are more of us about the house at the

172

weekend and Mr. Pickering, who has the two first-floor rooms, drew my attention to the fact that there were letters for Miss Frimwell still on the hallstand. Only circulars, of course — no one here receives very much correspondence. He also pointed out that he had not heard Miss Frimwell's radio, which she usually had on a good deal — quietly, of course, but ceilings are not soundproof. We knocked on her door and got no answer. It was unlocked, which was, I believe, unusual, for one likes to feel secure behind a locked door overnight if not during the day. Mr. Pickering and I went in and found her there in her chair." Mr. Sobieski paused and unobtrusively crossed himself.

After a moment Simpson asked, "Did you touch anything?"

"My dear young fellow, of course we did," said Mr. Sobieski. "What would you think we would do on entering the room and finding the poor lady dead, or at first thought, unconscious? We went to her, we tried to find signs of life. Then I telephoned for the ambulance."

"Not the police?"

"Why the police? The poor lady was old and frail and had died in her chair. And I am not clear now as to why you and your young colleagues have called on me."

"Just one or two loose ends, sir," said Simpson easily, "especially as there seems no next of kin, as I understand it."

"That I don't know. Certainly no one visited her, so far as I am aware. She did not leave us for Christmas or other festivities, and she had few letters. We are all somewhat solitary here, you understand — widowed or unmarried, no children. A house of ghosts." He smiled, his brown face like a walnut. Blane looked extremely suspicious.

"She had no visitors, you say, sir? None at all? No home helps, meals on wheels, district nurse?"

"Ah. The dog that did not bark in the night." Blane looked even more suspicious. "As to ordinary visitors I simply cannot say, as I have told you. I don't spend my days with an eye at the keyhole, watching my lodgers' comings and goings. She may have had some but I think it unlikely. As to functionaries from what are called the Social Services I can speak with more certainty. Miss Frimwell was an independent, able-bodied elderly lady, entirely able to look after herself. She did not need, no doubt would not accept, any of your so-called welfare benefits, as indeed I do not myself."

"She drew the pension, I suppose?"

"No doubt. We all do, of course. And are grateful."

A small chill silence enveloped them, broken by Sergeant Blane, who suddenly asked, "Pay her rent regular, did she?"

Mr. Sobieski turned his head a little to look at Blane.

"She did. Always."

"What day, sir?"

"Saturdays."

"Her decease was discovered Saturday. Had she paid already?"

"No. She usually did so on Saturday evenings. She would tap on my door, hand me the money in an envelope, I would make a note in her rent book, exchange a few courtesies, and that would be the end of the transaction. She would return to her small corner, and I to mine."

"You're a literary man, sir?" Simpson drew him back.

"I was. I was a lecturer in English literature at Cracow University in 1939. Since I became a British citizen I have busied myself with translations, journalism for the emigré press and such activities. They and this lodging-house have proved adequate."

"So she hadn't paid before her decease? You hadn't seen her?" Blane pushed in again.

"I have already said so."

"She wasn't expected till the evening, Sergeant," said Simpson. "Put it in your notes." He stood up. "Well, sir, I take it the room's not been touched? It's just as it was when the deceased was removed?"

"Certainly." Mr. Sobieski also rose. "Except, of course, that after she had been taken away, the next day when I had recovered a little, I went in and I dusted her poor things, Hoovered and tidied. It seemed only right, to leave all in order after her parting. To tell the truth . . ." He paused, sighing. "I have not quite known what to do, with no one coming forward to claim her belongings or take any responsibility for them. The situation is a strange one. In any case, I had sufficient regard for the lady not to wish to replace her before she is even in her grave. The funeral will be when?"

"That we don't quite know yet, sir. The post-mortem was only two days ago."

"Post-mortem?" Mr. Sobieski looked at him sharply. "What need? It was a natural death, surely?"

Simpson smiled reassuringly. "That's what we assumed, sir. But if a deceased person hasn't been seen by a doctor for two weeks prior to their death, then I'm afraid there has to be a post-mortem. And, as you say, Miss Frimwell seemed to be a tough old party —

176

if you'll pardon the expression." Blane looked shocked but Mr. Sobieski smiled. "She hadn't seen a doctor for months, as was ascertained from her NHS records. And now, sir, I wonder if you'd be good enough to let us see the room."

Sobieski stood up and from a drawer of the desk took a bunch of keys. He selected one, the rest dangling from his hand, and led them out into the passage and to the front-room door.

"You've kept it locked since her death, sir?"

"Of course."

He turned the key and the two policemen went inside, Sobieski looking in from the passage.

It was a good-sized room with shallow bay windows looking out on to the road, masked by net curtains. A small but solid table stood in the middle of the room, a coloured cloth over it; and between it and the fireplace was a big old wing chair. A divan in the corner with an afghan rug over it; a single-stemmed bedside table bearing nothing but an old, unwound alarm clock and a jar of Steradent; on the walls two framed certificates and a dark portrait of a bewhiskered clergyman; on the mantelpiece framed photographs — a group of First War VADs, some very young; a plump Edwardian lady entwined with two long-haired teenage girls; a majestic tabby cat. There were few books and those were stoutly bound old classics, looking as though not often opened, a Nevil Shute and a Dick Francis in large-print editions on the stool between chair and fireplace. On the chest of drawers with looking-glass above it, not very much. In the kitchenette behind a screen no dirty crocks, everything put away in its place.

The two men stood just inside the room and studied it. Then Simpson said, "It's just as it was when the deceased was removed, is it, sir? No one's been in since they took her away?"

"Only myself, as I told you. I was distressed — so good a lady, to have been sitting there dead, perhaps two days — so lonely. To put all in order seemed only right, out of respect for her. I locked the door as soon as I had finished. No one has been in since."

"Thank you, sir. We'll just have a look around and give you a shout when we're done."

Mr. Sobieski nodded and turned away. Simpson shut the door on him. "Right," he said. "Let's be having it."

It was sometime later that he sent Blane to ask Sobieski to come back to Miss Frimwell's room. He closed the door behind them and said, "Now, sir, I'd be obliged if you'd just stand here and have a good look around and tell me if the room looks like it ought."

The old man took a spectacle-case from the pocket of his jacket, opened it and put the glasses on. His hands trembled a little. His gaze circled the room carefully, pausing a moment on Blane, who stood with his back to the window making notes in his notebook.

"Most furniture is mine, a little of it was hers — the bedside table and the big chair."

"Everything looks normal?"

"I think so. Perhaps — yes, I think it is more bare. She had a clock — not that one on her bedside table, an antique one, glass and brass it was with a little handle, it stood on the mantelshelf and did not go. I think you call it a carriage clock? And where is her radio? A small transistor, it stood always here." He went round the table to the smaller one with the lamp and the large-print books on it. "And on the chest of drawers there she had a silver brush and a little box. Yes, I'm sure of it. These things were always there."

"Were they there when you and the other gentleman found her?"

He thought for a moment, frowning. "I can't say. I simply cannot say. We were concerned only for the poor lady, you see. We rushed in, we tried to revive her. We were not looking at her belongings."

"Not even when you returned from calling the ambulance?"

"Not even then."

"And the other gentleman?"

"Mr. Pickering was distressed. He is younger than I, he was not in the war. He was afraid of her when we knew she was dead and I sent him from the room."

"And what did you do then, sir?"

Sobieski was silent, looking at Simpson with steady eyes. "I said a prayer for the repose of her soul." At the window Blane looked shocked but Simpson nodded slightly. "I have seen a great deal of death. I knew almost at once that she had died quite a long time before, perhaps as much as twenty-four hours or so. I covered her with her shawl and said a prayer for her."

"Right you are, sir — understood. You didn't happen to notice if there was anything on the table beside her, did you — a cup and saucer, a glass, any kind of beverage?"

"There was nothing. As you see it now, the table was bare."

When he had gone Blane looked at Simpson smugly. "That clinches it then, doesn't it? A nice little Suspicious Death after all."

For the obligatory post-mortem reports had

shown that Sibyl Emily Frimwell, spinster, aged eighty-five and five months, had not died of a stroke or cancer or pneumonia or virus infection or any ailment symptomatic of old age but of an overdose of commonly pre- scribed sleeping pills; not many but strong ones, and too many for her little old body to accommodate. The report had landed on Simpson's desk, so here he was.

He looked round the tidy room, now bright with sunlight, and sighed. "Right," he said. "Rustle up Fingerprints. They're the only ones might find anything."

Simpson sat on a hard chair by the table and thought about Miss Frimwell dying in her chair opposite. He had sent Blane out for sandwiches and Coke, partly because it amused him to affront Blane's pomposity with such lowly errands, partly because he wanted to think within the quiet atmosphere of this room without Blane bustling about. He had been something like Blane once — but with a quick eye and a slick tongue, the human face of his guvnor, old Harry Hogarth, now made superintendent and due to retire in eigh- teen months, a hard man if ever there was one, massive and morose and not overparticu- lar in his methods. Simpson had been his ser- geant and his foil, the apprehension of villains a game to him while to Hogarth it had been a war. Blane would take after Hogarth but his weapons would be arrogance and the rule book. Blane was a real pill.

So Simpson sat alone with his elbows on the table and considered certain things. The old lady had sat in her chair opposite and died of too deep a sleep. It could be an Accidental. But there was no cup or glass beside her from which she had washed down the pills, nor in the alcove behind the screen in the corner where everything was put away or hanging neatly on its hooks. Had she swallowed the pills and tidied everything away before settling into her chair and waiting — for what? A snooze? Why should she take sleeping pills in the middle of the afternoon, which was when Forensic reckoned she had died? Where were the pills? Until the technical teams went over the place Simpson would not examine the room too closely, but he had seen nothing but some laxative and aspirin; and a half-full bottle of capsules labelled "One every four hours" — they didn't look like sleeping pills to him.

And where was her pension money, drawn the day before she was found, the rent not yet paid from it? Where was her carriage clock and her radio? Pawned? It did not seem likely from what he surmised of Miss Frimwell, but if so they would find the tickets.

They did not find the tickets. Nor did they find any of the small treasures old ladies might be expected to have, nor any cash. They found nothing but the bare bones of an old spinster's life. Scenes of Crimes found nothing either, thanks to Sobieski's Hoovering; and Fingerprints only those of Sobieski, Pickering and the ambulance men; not even many of Miss Frimwell's own. Surfaces had been well wiped. Who by, and when?

There were things to be done: check with the doctor named on her NHS card what, if any, prescriptions she had — Simpson would do that; check with the hospital where, from correspondence in the tidy desk, he had learned that Miss Frimwell did voluntary work — Blane could do that: check Pickering, the lodger from upstairs who had been with Sobieski when the body was discovered — Simpson again; check Fingerprints records, just in case — Blane; check neighbours for visitors, window-cleaners, itinerant traders, vagrants — Blane again; back at the station check Records for anything odd, any recurring pattern, a series of something not quite right — Simpson. For although he did not know what he was looking for he was pretty sure he would recognise it when he found it, and pretty sure that Blane would not.

He sent Blane off to the hospital where he did not think any useful information would be found, and himself called on Miss Frimwell's doctor, housed in a battered Victorian mansion, its insides catacombed into a series of rooms and cubbyholes, nest of a large group practice. Mid-afternoon was Family Planning clinic, and he waited self-consciously a few minutes among inquisitive-eyed young women and their push-chairs, fending off a toddler who kept thrusting a toy telephone into his ear.

From the doctor, a bearded fellow in a polo-necked sweater and track shoes, Simpson got Miss Frimwell's prescriptions and the opinion (from his records, for the doctor had so many old women patients he couldn't offhand remember Miss Frimwell by name) that she was as strong as a horse but could have gone any day.

"How d'you mean, sir?" asked Simpson.

The doctor flicked the buff card with his fingernail. "Arthritis, constipation, advancing cataract — nothing we won't all of us have, give or take a year or so. And angina — she'd had an attack or two but none for the last six months. She had some tablets for that — yes, those are the ones," as Simpson showed him the bottle he had found. "But nothing else.

And she'd not been to the surgery since —
when?" He studied the card again, "Last No-
vember. I remember her now, I think — tough
little old girl. Very polite, always dressed just
so — what used to be called a lady." He
grinned deep in his beard. "Not many like
that around. One less now, of course."

"You never prescribed sleeping pills, tran-
quillizers?"

"Nope, nothing like that. Her sort don't hold
with that kind of thing."

"But her heart . . . ?"

"Any time, given overload. She was an old
lady. That's why I must say I'm surprised at
you lot being interested. I'd've thought natural causes, open and shut. But you say the
post-mortem . . ." He looked perplexed, laying
the card face down beside the stethoscope and
the blood pressure machine. "Well, nothing
I prescribed for her could have caused it. Absolutely not. Whatever your lab chaps found,
it wasn't from me."

Simpson was tired. He walked back to the
station through the humid later afternoon
and wished he were somewhere else. The
High Street, too narrow for its flood of traffic,
depressed him with its pavements still un-
mended from the winter frosts, its empty
shops mouldering behind dirty windows, its

open ones shabby or glittering plastic, more videos than groceries, building societies than butchers. The people he passed seemed alien; even the young mums in the clinic had been withdrawn behind their eyes or their babies; people no longer seemed to look into anyone else's eyes but remained closed behind their own. If they knew he was the law they would become hostile or nervous; they didn't see him as a source of help in whatever troubles they might have, but would be resentful of him or resigned.

Why had he joined the police? He could have chosen to become a forester or a keeper in the zoo, a market gardener or an attendant in a stately home. Anything but a detective inspector on a stuffy London afternoon at rush hour, wondering why a little old lady had died in her chair, not from her ailments but from too much of what had never been prescribed.

Back in the clinical disorder of the station Blane was full of himself. Sipping a mug of tea, he read his notes aloud to Simpson with the complacency of an after-dinner speaker. Everything he had learned at the hospital was unimportant: Miss Frimwell had gone there every Monday and Wednesday mornings from ten o'clock till twelve to help prepare dressings, unpaid and rather an embarrassment to the department, for her arthritis made her slow and they would have got on better without her. But she had trained at the hospital many years ago and worked there all through her prime, coming in after the First War, in which she had been a very young VAD. Her bonds with the hospital were strong, she had always declared she felt herself part of the team still, and while there was anything she could usefully do the department had not had the heart to stop her coming.

They had all liked and admired her. She had been courteous, incisive and intelligent, even though age had slowed her down a bit. Although her body was frail her spirit was resolute. Growing smaller, lighter and whiter over the years, a little old scrap of steely thistledown, she had maintained the well-mannered integrity of the Edwardian age into which she had been born.

None of them knew anything else about her. She had never talked about family or friends, only sometimes reminisced about colleagues of her younger days. She had never referred to her physical condition, although it was understood she had to be careful of her heart. She could have had no access to drugs of any kind at the hospital, was never anywhere near them even if it were conceivable that she should want them.

"That's about it, sir," Blane concluded, closing his notebook with a smirk.

"Ta very much." Simpson slumped down in his chair and shut his eyes. "A basinful of fuck-all."

"Even negative information is of use." Blane slid the notebook back into his breast pocket and finished his tea.

"Elimination. Like All-Bran."

"It narrows the field. The provenance of the toxic substance seems to be the priority."

Simpson gave him a sour look. "Where did she get the stuff, you mean?" He sat upright, hunching his shoulders. "If it wasn't from the hospital and it wasn't prescribed, then she either got it herself — which I don't believe — or someone slipped it to her."

"Pickering. Chap on the first floor, sir. He works part-time in the chemist's she got her prescription from. I checked all the local pharmacies after I left the hospital, as you instructed, and in any case the label's on the container for her tablets. I also ascertained from the manager that's where she always got them — they knew her well, apart from checking up their records. Pickering was on duty Thursday."

"But he wasn't left alone with the body."

"We have only the foreign gentleman's word for that at this moment in time. He might have found means to eliminate all traces of the event."

"In those few minutes?"

"We don't know how long the Polish gentleman was absent. And Pickering was on duty at the pharmacist's on Thursday morning, early closing, nine to one. All day Friday and Saturday too." Blane looked smug. "I didn't take enquiries further until I had your instructions."

Simpson pulled himself upright. "Shit — I'd hoped we could call it a day. Best give him a call, then. He ought to be in now."

There was a light on behind the drawn curtains of the first-floor front windows when Simpson and Blane returned to Sobieski's house and rang the front door bell twice, as instructed on the card.

Mr. Pickering was short, fat and shiny, his round pink ball of a head balanced on the round larger ball of a body. Over an ordinary shirt and trousers he wore a short Japanese dressing-gown on the back of which they could see, as he led them up the stairs, an aggressive dragon embroidered in gold thread that was fraying a bit. Simpson noticed the prejudices forming in the lift of Blane's eyebrows as they followed up to the first floor and into Pickering's rooms.

Pickering was flustered, and bounced about offering them a variety of seats in a room stuffed full of stuffed furniture. Buttoned, bow-legged and braided pieces almost hid the Turkey carpet; bobbled plush hid the mantelshelf and the table, framed the windows, in which stood a rolltop desk. The walls were hung with engravings and reproductions of pictures from the turn of the century, mostly of children — sentimental subjects, arms entwined round dogs, cradling kittens, cuddling up to a cradle. There was much bric-à-brac and this too was of the same kind: pink and white figurines with frilled skirts and baskets of flowers, shepherdesses with adoring sheep, a nymph or two seemingly modest in china drapery, sprouting little wings and gazing into china pools, sporting bows and arrows or playing the flute. On the mantelpiece, between two vases of dried flowers and a double leather frame containing photographs of three long-haired, flounced schoolgirls clasped decorously together, was a brass carriage clock.

Pickering fussed about, offering them tea, coffee, lemonade, his pop-eyed gaze rolling from one to the other in, it seemed, a frenzy of apprehension. To calm him Simpson accepted some lemonade and sat on one of the buttoned chairs, but Blane remained aloof and standing, his hands behind his back like a constable on duty, studying and remembering every object in the room.

With Pickering at last at rest on the edge of a love-seat, Simpson explained their presence. "It's not right, you see, sir, that our old folk should be allowed to pass away without anyone knowing, like this poor lady did, and it's felt that enquiries ought to be made into the quality of social care, questions of neglect, gaps in the welfare net, that sort of thing."

"Quite, quite. I absolutely agree."

"We pride ourselves on being a caring society and yet something of this kind can happen, right in our midst." He shook his head sadly and Pickering drooped. "So we wondered if you had any idea of what visitors she had, if any. Services like meals on wheels, district nurse, that sort of thing?"

"Oh dear me no, I'm afraid I can't help you at all." His eyes rolled in anguish towards the impassive Blane. "We keep ourselves very much to ourselves in this house, it's one of the great advantages — no knocking on doors, borrowing sugar, dropping in. We respect our privacy and really, apart from Miss Frimwell and Mr. Sobieski, I couldn't be sure I'd recognise any of the other tenants, not unless I saw them coming out of their rooms. I only knew Miss Frimwell because we sometimes took our milk in at the same time — and once or twice I did have to knock on her door and ask her to turn her radio down. She was rather deaf, you see, and just underneath me here."

"Did she resent that, sir?"

"Oh dear me no, not at all. She was a perfect lady, quiet as a mouse except on those few occasions when she hadn't realised the volume . . . I hardly ever saw her."

"So you've no idea if she had any visitors?"

"None at all, I'm afraid. I never heard any. But then I'm out a good deal. And of course, she went to the hospital some days a week, I don't know which, voluntary work, I believe."

"How d'you know that, then?" asked Blane.

"Mr. Sobieski must have mentioned it. Or perhaps she did herself, in passing, perhaps. I really can't remember."

"You'd have an interest, though, wouldn't you, her working at the hospital and you at the pharmacist's?"

Pickering's round head flushed to its polished top. "Pure coincidence, pure coincidence. We never mentioned it, never. I believe all she did was help prepare dressings, nothing at all to do with pharmacy. Nothing at all."

Simpson said, "You're a qualified pharmacist, are you, sir? I understood so from Mr. Sobieski."

"That is correct. But I only work part-time

— I have a disability, a full-time job is too much for me. I work half-days Thursday, whole days Friday and Saturday."

"So you'd be in on the day we believe Miss Frimwell died?"

"Oh dear — yes, I would, in the afternoon. If you think it was Thursday."

"Who made up her prescriptions?" Blane demanded.

"Her prescriptions?" Hands clasped as eyes rolled again. "I've no idea."

"Brought them to your shop, didn't she?"

"I believe so. She may have done. It's the nearest."

"So who made them up?"

"Anyone. All of us. If she did."

"Take it from me, she did. We've checked the records. So what did she take?"

"I've no idea. If you've seen the records you must know."

"But you'd know too."

"I make up scores of prescriptions in a single day. I have no idea whatever who they're for and would certainly not remember what they were of."

Simpson broke in, finishing his glass of lemonade, which had been extremely diluted, and leaning towards Pickering with a confidential air. "The trouble is, sir, we can't trace any prescriptions or medicines which might account for the old lady's death. The records at your shop show she had tablets for this and that but nothing that quite fits the bill for us, d'you see? So we wondered, just off the top of our heads like, if there was ever a possibility she might have got hold of something of that nature from you, sir? Quite by chance, as it were?"

Pickering went white this time. "Certainly not!"

"Like as if she might have mentioned casually one day, as you're both taking in your milk, that she's not sleeping well or has anxiety spells or some such, and you might have said you'd got just the thing as might help, a sample or a tail end of one of your own, anything like that, and passed it over to her and thought no more about it?" He paused encouragingly. "Something like that?"

"Certainly not," repeated Pickering faintly.

"Mind if I have a look around?" said Blane after a moment's silence. "You've some nice things here."

Against squeaks from Pickering he moved inexorably towards the double doors between the two rooms, opened one and went into the bedroom. Simpson followed him, giving Pickering a cheery smile as he went, and almost bumped into Blane, who stood transfixed just inside the doorway.

Although the room was dark, light from the front room was enough for them to see that this was even more of a shrine to Victorian childhood than the other, for not only were the walls thickly hung with sentimental pictures of the same kind, the furniture similarly bobbled and plushed, flowery toiletries, even a ring tree, on the dressing-table, but seated in the one chair and lying with thickly fringed closed eyelids on the bed were several almost child-sized china dolls. They had long hair and two of them wore sun-bonnets. All of them were dressed in starched and spotless petticoats, drawers and dresses, kid shoes on their small feet, their dimpled hands half-raised from their skirts as though in welcome.

"Strewth!" hissed Blane.

Pickering fussed at their backs. "I'm a collector. My sisters started them. So nostalgic . . . I was the youngest, the only son. These were handed down, our mother — just the smallest two. Then I began collecting. It's quite profitable, you know, quite a market."

"Sell them, do you?"

"Oh no! No, I don't sell them, I collect them. A hobby. Quite fascinating." He seemed to be wringing his hands.

Blane had overcome his amazement and was moving about the room scrutinising but not touching anything, disapproval in every gesture.

Simpson turned back into the sitting-room. "Worth a bob or two I expect by now, sir. Amazing the things that fetch money nowadays — bottle tops, beer mats, Dinky cars. If I had a bob for every Dinky car I had when I was a kid I'd be living in the Bahamas. Did Miss Frimwell like your collection?"

"Miss Frimwell? No, she never saw it, she never came up here."

"Have any of her own, did she?"

"I've told you, I hardly knew her."

"They'd be about her period, I'd have said. She might have had a dolly of her own tucked away somewhere."

"No, no, I'm sure not!"

"How, sir?"

"How what?"

"How are you sure, if you never had nothing to do with her?"

Pickering's pate seemed shinier than ever. "I'm not sure! What I mean is simply I don't think so. I wouldn't know, naturally. The subject never came up, we never really spoke. She might have had, from her own childhood. But I certainly have no idea, no idea at all."

"You'd be interested if she had, though, wouldn't you," declared Blane, emerging from the bedroom with an air of disdain.

"Yes I would — of course I would. But I've no reason to suppose . . . I've really no idea."

"They're all yours, are they? Had them for years?"

"Yes. Yes I have." He was really wringing his hands now.

"The trouble is, you see, sir, we don't really know what the poor lady had," Simpson took over again, "and that's complicated, see, should there be any next of kin. What we do know is she had a very nice carriage clock." He allowed his gaze to move towards the mantelshelf.

Mr. Pickering was like a marshmallow, alternately white and pink. Now he was white. "You don't think — you're not implying . . . ?"

"We're not implying anything, sir, just stating a fact. We know she possessed a carriage clock and that's gone missing. It could be that while she was falling asleep, or dead even, someone slipped in and nicked it."

"Had yours long, have you? An heirloom like the dollies?" sneered Blane.

Pickering sat down suddenly on a hard chair and looked at them in anguish. "I assure you . . . What can I say? I've had it for years, it belonged to my parents, a wedding present, before the First War. For years."

"And you never, as you might say, loaned

the old lady a pill or two, something to help her sleep, nothing like that?" Simpson smiled.

"Nothing. I've told you. Nothing whatever at any time, never. I was never inside her room except then, when we found her. Never." He stared at them, pink and glistening and hopeless.

"You've been very helpful, sir." Simpson moved briskly to the door, Blane following. "It might just be we might send the fingerprint lads round to check out the clock — just for elimination. Or, tell you what, if you've no objection, we'll take it along with us now. I'll give a receipt, of course." While Pickering sat silent Simpson nodded to Blane, who, moving back to the fireplace, brought out a handkerchief and delicately swathed the clock in it. "You shall have it back in a day or two," said Simpson, making out the receipt and laying it on the table, "and I'll try and make sure it's kept wound up. A nice clock like that needs taking care of."

With a smile and a wave, he took Blane away, Pickering remaining stunned in his chair.

As they closed the front door behind them Blane said, "Christ, what a weirdo!"

"Poor sod. It's little girls is his trouble, I

reckon, not little old ladies. Still, give the prints a whirl, see what they say."

They got into the car and drove down the now dark street towards the lights and traffic of the main road. Depression clamped down on Simpson: the sad frightened freak they had just left, the sad solitary old bat who had died, as alone then as apparently in her life; the fact that everything had been wiped clean, no fingerprints save those of people who had come after her death, nothing for Scenes of Crime men because of Sobieski's respect for the dead, and because no one had thought a crime had been committed until too long had passed; the fact that they were getting nowhere.

They would have to check again house-to-house if anyone had seen callers — but they never had, and they'd said so already when Blane went round the first day. Still, got to do something . . .

The vision of that little old lady, sitting dead in her chair while the world went on outside, upset Simpson. Death had begun to upset him lately, the insult of it — violent death, that was.

And violent death was what had come to eighty-five-year-old Sibyl Emily Frimwell, no matter how peacefully she'd sat in her chair. Someone had fed her those pills and taken her treasures. And Simpson would get them. Maybe.

He parted from Blane and found a callbox, listened to the ring, pressed the button. "That you, love? Sorry I couldn't make it, I got put on the emergency shift. Yeah, well, never mind, I'll come over now, okay? Yeah, anything, pizza, whatever. Yeah, I know. I'll be there in ten minutes. See ya, Jan."

7

When Janice had returned from her evening with Dave ten days before and found Grace's note on the table, she had flopped down in the nearest chair as though her legs had given way. Her first thought, after her stomach had given a great plunge and then righted itself, was How am I going to manage? Shock had blanked out Grace's information that the rent was paid to the end of the month, and all she could think of for the moment was that she had a few pounds in her purse and her wages from Mr. Theodore and nothing else between her and the hostile world. She sat stunned, emptied as though by a sluice of everything but panic.

Then she got angry in a feeble sort of way. The cow, the bloody cow! Running out on her like that without so much as a hint, after all these months together and Jan working with her on the old people set-up that would never have worked without the two of them: a team they'd been, working in with each other as smooth as smooth and never a hitch. But Grace had been the brains of it, Janice knew that, and on her own what was to become of her?

She got to her feet and went into the bedroom half of the room to poke about in the wardrobe and the drawers. Nothing of hers was missing. Grace had removed only her own belongings, but had taken the two suitcases that had been stored on top of the wardrobe and a zip-up bag they had sometimes used when selling off their acquisitions. She did not seem even to have investigated Janice's things, for two or three little pieces of jewellery to which Janice had taken a fancy over the months they had worked together were still wrapped safely in their kleenex and hidden at the back of the drawer where she kept her bras and briefs and Tampax. So Grace had borne her no ill will — nor good will either. She had, like everyone in Janice's experience, simply moved on.

But what was she to do? She was safe till the end of the month, the place was hers for another two weeks or so. And a spurt of joy suddenly went through her, for it was hers alone now and Dave could come here! They could go to bed here in the sags and hollows where she and Grace had slept divided, they could be together like a real couple, no more back seats or grass or longed-for but never repeated hotel bedroom, but here in her own place now Grace had gone!

Dave! How could she have forgotten Dave? Dave would help her. He would tease her and help her and go to bed with her. She would heat up tasty snacks for him. And perhaps, in the snugness of her own place, eating Chinese or Indian takeaways, going to bed in the big bed, he would want to stay with her a bit — not for ever, of course, not married or anything like that, that was too much of a dream — but for a bit, for a few months, for longer than if they'd had to go on with nowhere proper to have sex in.

She went into the front half of the room, and plugged in the kettle for a mug of coffee. Dave! She wanted to tell him, now, at once. "Dave," she'd say, "Auntie had to go north. Her sister's ill. She won't be back and I'm here on my own. It's our room now, Dave. I'll make you some beans on toast. It's number 44, just push the front door open and it's the door on the left. As soon as you can, Dave. . . ."

But then she sagged again. For he was working tonight, she wouldn't see him till tomorrow in the King's Crown as usual, if he wasn't on sudden call, and there was no way she could contact him before then.

She had no phone number for him, no address, she did not even know where he worked. She had resigned herself to that, as she had resigned herself to everything that had ever happened to her, from Uncle Charley onwards, but it was sad. She would so like to share her joy with him now, this minute, to ring him and say, "Come round, come now, come to bed," to see him push open the door and look round, smiling the quizzing sort of way he had, to put her arms round him and smell his smell and feel his mouth and his cock getting hard and fall on to the bed and not get out of it till morning. . . .

But she couldn't. She had no way of reaching him. It had been quite a time before she had even known his last name, for no one bothered with last names nowadays. Simpson, it was — Dave Simpson. . . .

Dave Simpson had shared a flat for a couple of years with "Porky" Waller, a cheerful fellow from the Serious Crimes squad — it was Porky they had run into at Speakers' Corner that weekend, and Simpson had been nervous Porky would give the game away that they were coppers, for he knew from experience that nothing turned some girls off quicker than that. But Porky had got the message.

The three boxlike rooms of their flat were comfortable if characterless — neither man had either the time or inclination for home-making; the shared living room (in which they seldom lived) held a television set, a lumpy sofa and armchairs, a lot of paperbacks (thrillers and adventure), discarded newspapers, *Playboy* and *Private Eye*. Porky's bedroom was a confusion of clothes, bedclothes, ashtrays, shoes, and smelled of them all, plus an underlay of stale perfumes; Simpson's was tidy, his clothes on hangers, the floor clear, the window locked open a permanent three inches.

In and out of Porky's room went a succession of women, full-blown rather than slender, with manes of hair rather than cropped-short spikes, heavy scents and bangles and earrings. None of them lasted long, but Simpson never knew whether one of them was in there with Porky when he came home, not unless he could hear them — the apartment block put up in the euphoria of Swinging Britain was anything but soundproof. If Porky didn't mind (and he didn't), Simpson didn't; but he didn't fancy conducting his own affairs in so open a manner. When they first moved into the flat he had sometimes brought a girl back; there were plenty around if you weren't too choosy and at that stage he wasn't. But a year or so ago he'd fallen heavily for Lisa; he'd been really serious, looked into the future, seen a semi, kids, a superintendentship. But she'd hated his job — the long uncertain hours, the drudgery, the occasional danger and the dragging sordidness of the world in which he worked. She'd walked away from him and he'd made the decision never to get too serious again — and never to let on what his job was. Being a policeman was like being a clergyman — it turned people off. He'd become as close-shut against outsiders as a clam.

After Lisa he hadn't the taste for casual pickups any more. He was older and getting more fastidious, amused by Porky's antics but beginning to be sickened a little by the mean and pitiful lives with which his work brought him in contact. His father had been a schoolmaster, an idealist, all of whose geese were swans until they vandalised the gym, sniffed glue in the latrines, made obscene drawings in their textbooks, grew taller and stronger than he and left school for the streets at sixteen. Even then he believed in them; still did, living in Hove in sheltered housing, growing deaf.

His mother had been a Christian Scientist who died of asthma when Dave was seventeen. He had never forgiven her for her suffering, nor his father for his acquiescence. He wanted order, action, justice. He joined the police.

He believed in his job; he believed in order, and the law was to enforce it. He had believed in the worth of people, as his parents had taught him; but that belief had not much helped either of them, their trust had got them nowhere. He enjoyed the comradeship of the force, the partnerships and shared action, the functional brightness of the station, the give and take of male companionship; but one or two of them lately had made him uneasy. He had not joined the police force to become a bully, nor to see the mean and savage multiply beyond the possibility of justice, nor to be powerless to protect the weak. He was, if he thought about it (and lately he quite often did) as much of an idealist and in error as his parents. Behind his easy, confident façade he was becoming more and more a troubled and a private man, taking what came his way, the rough with the smooth, the brutal with the pathetic, not committing himself, but musing . . .

Janice was one of the things that had come his way.

His first reaction when an unusually animated Janice had told him, in the King's Crown that Thursday evening nearly a week ago, that her aunt had been called north to a sick relative and that the bed-sit was now theirs, had been consternation. Even though the inconveniences of al fresco or back-seat sex were considerable, at least it kept him free, almost anonymous; and although he liked to give pleasure as well as to receive it, he was not all that bothered as to its surroundings. In fact, had Janice not drifted across his path those weeks ago, when he'd been off his usual patch visiting a mate from another division who had been badly injured trying to stop a smash-and-grab robbery, had she not so obviously been available so that not to accept her would have been not only daft (never refuse an offer) but offensive, he would never have got into a relationship with her at all. She hadn't exactly raped him; but her almost naïve assumption that sex was what he required of her had led him to go along with it as much out of kindness of heart as active desire. It had been O.K. nothing great, a routine exercise which had its conveniences. But after Lisa he had rather lost the taste for sex without love.

Janice hung around, hung on; she accepted his non-arrivals, asked no questions, expected him to use her yet, in a way he found oddly touching, also expected him to drop her. She asked nothing of him, simply hoped; was not curious about his life, simply accepted that she had no place in it.

Bit by bit he had found himself engaged by her very passivity. She was a born no-hoper and something in him, some vestige of his parents' useless idealism, some latent disgust at the mean and meagre criminals he met within his daily work, teased him to make something of her. He hardly at all believed the stories she had told him of her past — he recognised phoney fantasies when he heard them, as he did a dozen times a week in his job — and guessed but did not want to know that she lived shadily on the fringes of the welfare state. But he did believe that she lived with her auntie, for once, in their early days, intrigued by the way she made him drop her off at the street corner, he had almost idly checked out her address. He had driven round the block, picked up her figure walking down the street, turning in; had come back another day when he was off duty, parked and waited a while, seen her come out of the house with an older, neatly dressed woman. And he did believe, almost unwillingly, that somewhere within her feckless, timid personality was the possibility of joy.

He knew that he was being stupid. What he should do was cut and run, kindly if possible but do it anyway. Yet the hotel weekend they had spent together, a quixotic gesture on his part that had astonished him at the time, had given him something too; not only the gratification of her tremendous, surely first ever orgasm and the bondage it had laid upon her, but a wish to see her well, to enrich her and so, perhaps, himself.

Nevertheless, the fact that now she was on her own and that, short of dropping her, there was no way in which he could avoid being more closely involved, alarmed him. He had managed to keep her distanced out of his life but now could not avoid entering more closely into hers. But, no doubt about it, a bed-sit with a nice big bed and her fussing about, coming on domestic (with no more sense of how to fry an egg than fight Star Wars) was better than the back of a car. He could drop in when he came off work, whatever time that was, for she'd given him a key. She was always there, always grateful that he'd come. And it had stopped her asking questions. She was so proud of it all — the room, him. And the sex — he had to admit that the sex, in the big doublebed, had surprised him. She had screamed, he had groaned. He had almost loved her. With some apprehension, he was pretty sure that she certainly loved him. . . .

8

Mrs. Robinson was still in bed when Grace arrived with her suitcases, and Conroy almost had tears in his eyes as he settled her into the rather clammy small room, hitherto used for storage, now adapted for Grace. During the time between his mother's fall and the agreement with and arrival of Grace, he had been forced to take several days off from his office, as their domestic help had left without notice rather than carry trays to and from the bedside and help with toilet problems. In desperation he had contacted the Social Services, who had sent a bad-tempered black lady to give Mrs. Robinson a bath and a bad-tempered white lady who consented to do some shopping but would not Hoover the carpets.

"It's so very good of you," he said to Grace, having brought in her suitcases, "I'm afraid it's not very . . ."

"Don't you fret. It'll do me fine." There was just room for a divan (it had been Conroy's when a lad), and a dressing-table had been contrived out of piled-up luggage (including a trunk marked MARION CONROY in large white letters) covered by a tablecloth. There were hooks and hangers behind the door, and he offered her the cupboard in the hall from which he had cleared his own outdoor clothing. "How's your mother? Has she seen the doctor?"

"She won't." His ruddy cheeks sagged and he seemed to have lost weight even in these few days.

"Oh, we can't have that. You ring him up straight away and get him to take a look." For Grace had learned long ago that it always paid to be on the right side of doctors, and those who attended the old people's homes had invariably admired her cheerful efficiency.

The Robinsons' doctor also; he changed the blood-pressure pills, ordered a walking-frame, and spoke of the danger of bedsores if a woman of Mrs. Robinson's weight remained in bed too long.

Grace gravely agreed. They parted with mutual confidence that they need not meet again.

Her fall had certainly taken some of the bounce out of Mrs. Robinson. She had lost weight and had shrunk a bit, partly because she was now afraid to stand up straight, preferring to hunch over her walking-frame, for that way she felt there was less far to fall should she do so again. "That's right, dear, take it slowly. Hold tight, that's the way," said Grace, hovering behind her ready to catch as Mrs. Robinson crept down the passage and across into her chair. There she lay back, panting, and closed her eyes, but opened them again as Grace tucked a rug over her knees to give her a glare behind which lurked fear.

"I should like a cup of Bovril," she commanded.

"Just the thing," smiled Grace, going towards the kitchen.

"And I'll take a little sherry in it — I'll add that myself."

"Rightyo."

Grace waited for the kettle to boil, humming a tune from *King and I*. Everything was in her own hands: The nursing and the home-help ladies had been dismissed, for she had pointed out to Conroy that now he had a live-in housekeeper he was not entitled to them. He had gazed at her for a moment before replying, "Are you sure it's not too much for you? All the nursing as well?"

"Nonsense. It's not nursing she needs, just a bit of help here and there and an eye kept on her. To tell you the truth, I'd rather not have anyone else about, interfering." Which was true.

She moved very carefully; it was a game

she liked playing. With Mrs. Robinson she was subservient but composed. She helped her to the lavatory, brought her breakfast on a tray, while Conroy, relieved of these chores, ate his silently behind the *Daily Telegraph* in the kitchen. Grace had her own breakfast after he had gone, with Radio 4 for company. After the washing-up, the tidy-up and the Hoovering, came the old lady's toilet; this took time, help with washing and dressing, banished while make-up and hair were arranged, then the querulous crawl to the sitting-room, the elevenses. After that Grace went out — to the shops or just for a walk around or a cup of coffee in one of the many cafés, watching the people, sometimes browsing in the post offices and betting shops and public libraries, just for old times' sake. Back to a light lunch for the two of them and listen to the old girl's monologue, which dwelt more and more on the past as her confidence in the present faltered. Then the crawl down the passage again, lavatory, up on the bed with a hot-water bottle, silence till tea-time. Sometimes Grace went out again when Mrs. Robinson was safely asleep; but mostly she made herself comfortable in the sitting-room, and for the first few days after her arrival went carefully through every drawer, desk and cupboard in the flat. Those that were locked did not present much difficulty; only one baffled her, a black japanned box in the bottom of Conroy's wardrobe. She would master it in time.

She did not learn very much; the Robinsons were what they seemed to be, and much of the stuff she rifled through was old programmes, photographs, press cuttings. There was some nice silver, and although she never had long alone in Mrs. Robinson's bedroom there was some decent jewellery, nothing special but nice enough and worth a pound or two. The best thing was on the old girl's finger, a ruby and diamond worn over the wide wedding ring under the knobbed knuckle. She liked to wear a nice gold chain too, with a pendant on it, Victorian chased. It all added up.

He had some nice things as well: real ivory brushes, a set of pearl dress studs, a silver flask and cigar case (initials not his, his father's, most like), cuff-links — no one wore those any more. He had a hundred pounds in cash tucked away in his socks; and the old girl had too, under her thermal underwear.

There was tea to be served and eaten, the six o'clock news on TV. On weekdays Grace cooked the supper, and poured Conroy's whisky when he got home, leaving mother and son alone together while she finished and served the meal. Mostly they all watched telly afterwards until the long haul of getting Mrs. Robinson back into bed; but the second week Grace was there Conroy went out on the Wednesday evening, with a sour look from his mother, and Grace heard him come home just after midnight. He had got to his feet, pulled down his waistcoat, said, "Well, I think I'll just go out for a breather," given his mother a kiss on her hostile cheek, nodded to Grace and gone. Grace had looked enquiringly at Mrs. Robinson, but the old lady had just sat there looking like thunder and her lips tight shut, and the repeat of "Tenku" came on, so nothing was said.

At the weekends Conroy did the cooking. He was good at it and enjoyed it; and as an elderly couple, younger than Mrs. Robinson but dating from theatre days, came in to play bridge every Saturday evening it was assumed that Grace was off duty. She found this rather a bore; she had nowhere to go and had never liked spending money. Now she had to pay for a seat at the cinema, buy herself a meal, or sit alone with one gin and vermouth in a pub somewhere, sometimes getting into a conversation but always disengaging herself with composure before closing time. It was dead boring. She even missed Janice and her lackadaisical chat. She certainly missed the planning, tracking and carrying out of her old occupation; the calculation, the marking of the subject, the excitement and power of the call, the spiel, the subjugation, the gathering up, the walking away, the confirmation that she was in control of them, of Janice, of herself. She missed too the wary give and take of her "outlets," the sharp-eyed old men in dusty shops, the hard-eyed younger men or women on the antique stalls. Still, if her plans worked out right, it would be worth it.

She made a point of being back before the Lorings left, coming in with a smile and an offer to make tea, impressing them with her gentility, and withdrawing to her own room until they were leaving when, with another smile and a cheery word, she came out to help them with their coats. Wendy Loring had played the teenage daughter in "Nanny Jane's Journal" until she was in her sixties, possessing a light voice which did not age and which came strangely out of the dumpy, white-haired woman she had become, a little deaf but well rouged and eye-shadowed over her soft skin. Dickie had been box office manager of a West End theatre most of his life and still carried an air of being always in evening dress — those were the days! Small and dapper, hair and moustache white, he was still a ladies' man, buttering up Mrs. Robinson under his wife's indulgent eye, shaking Grace's hand in farewell with a meaning look that meant nothing. They possessed a well-tended Mini and as they drove away the first Saturday evening he said, "That housekeeper's a tough cookie. Maybe Marion's met her match this time."

"Poor Conroy," his wife answered absently. "What a life!"

But as the days passed Conroy seemed very content. Although his demeanour did not change nor his face become more animated, there seemed a warmer glow behind his heavy façade, a relaxation which, if he had allowed it, might have seemed almost boyish. He never failed to express his gratitude to Grace as each Saturday morning he awkwardly handed her the envelope containing her wages — with embarrassment on his side they had agreed on a sum which, plus her board and lodging, would see her through, she reckoned, for the time being. He did not speak much but, with Mrs. Robinson and the television, there was no need. On Saturdays he went shopping for the weekend meals, brought back flowers for his mother and claret from Sainsbury's wine department. If the weather were fine, he walked in Kensington Gardens. On Sundays he read the *Sunday Telegraph* and did the crossword with his mother, withdrew to his own room after lunch for what Grace assumed must be a nap. He went out after supper but did not invite Grace to accompany him; nor on those Wednesdays, which Grace found were ritual and which remained unexplained.

This was not what Grace had planned.

"I do think it's wonderful the way your son loves his home," she said on Saturday while Conroy was in the kitchen unpacking the results of his shopping and Grace was easing his mother into her chair, her toilet completed. "It's not many men take such an interest. I know my hubby, bless him, he just loved to be out and about — shows, clubs, coach trips, you couldn't hardly keep him at home."

"Careful! Oh dear!" Mrs. Robinson subsided into her chair, breathing hard, necklace swinging over the prow of her bosom. "The cushion — it's in the wrong place." Grace adjusted it. "Is a window open? I feel a draught." Grace went and closed it. "I left my spectacles in the bedroom. Has the *Radio Times* come?"

Grace fetched them both. "There you are, dear. Your son's just putting the shopping away. You certainly brought him up to be a real home-lover."

"Yes, well, he was at boarding-school and I was away so much. Not in the later years, of course, we used just to rehearse and record

219

at BH the three days a week. But by then Conroy was away from home. . . ." Her voice trailed away.

"That'd be on his national service?" She tucked the rug over Mrs. Robinson's knees.

"Yes it was — and later, for a few years, before he came home again."

"He was off later, then, was he?"

"For a few years." Mrs. Robinson's lips closed firmly and she picked up the *Radio Times*.

"It's nice when they love their homes, it's a tribute to their parents, I always say." She moved the Zimmer frame to one side, clicking up the facts in her head. "I expect going out in the evenings now and then as he does he appreciates it all the more. Does he have a hobby? I think it's nice when men have a hobby, like billiards and stamps and that."

"He plays bridge. He goes to his bridge club on Wednesdays and plays bridge."

"That's ever such a brainy game, isn't it. But of course he is brainy, anyone can see that."

"Yes Conroy is certainly 'brainy.'" Mrs. Robinson put the word in inverted commas with a patronising smile and opened the journal. Grace had gone far enough.

So if it was bridge on Wednesdays what was it on Sundays? Did he still go to the Old

George and sit alone with a bottle of wine? She decided to ask him.

Within the intimacy of the kitchen a dignified camaraderie had developed between them. She had asked him to call her Grace, although in front of his mother she was still Mrs. Black; and he had reciprocated by offering his own Christian name, which Grace would never allow past her lips outside the kitchen. So she felt it would not be ill-judged if she were to make the first, carefully considered advance. As she scraped potatoes for him and he carefully supervised the slow thickening of a sauce, she asked, "Do you still go up west on Sunday?"

"Yes."

"To the dear Old George? I must say I miss it. There was such a nice class of people there, wasn't there, nothing rowdy ever and the music just a nice background, not too loud."

"Yes."

"It's still the same, is it?" It was like pulling teeth!

"Yes, much the same." His back was as impassive as she knew his front would be.

"I must say I'd really like a drink out in a nice pub again of a Sunday. It somehow marks off the weekend, doesn't it?"

"Well, I'd be delighted . . . I mean, I never thought, since you've been here, I mean

". . ." He turned, still stirring the contents of the pan, his expression mildly embarrassed.

She laughed charmingly. "Oh goodness, no, I don't mean going up west. I'd not want to leave your mother too long, not on a Sunday, now she's used to my company. But I must say I'd really enjoy slipping out somewhere local. There must be some nice quiet place nearby?"

"Yes. Yes, there must be." He turned back to the stove.

"Of course, I wouldn't want to go on my own. Not at first, anyway. I'll have to pocket my pride and ask you to escort me, Conroy."

"Well, yes, delighted. Remiss of me."

Mrs. Robinson took it very badly. She sat hunched down in her chair when Conroy told her they were going out for an hour or so, her large face, so like her son's, sullen beneath its jetty casque (a hairdresser came every fortnight to shampoo, set and touch up the roots, Grace being shut from the bedroom while this rite was carried out).

"Grace is here as my companion," she growled. "It's not right that I should be left."

"It's just for an hour, Mother. You'll be all right."

"Anything might happen — I might fall."

"You're not to move out of your chair, dear, that you must promise me."

"You were safe enough on your own, before Mrs. Black joined us."

"That was before I had my fall. You don't realize how that fall shook me up."

"It's only for an hour, Mother. Just round the corner."

"Not up west?"

"No, no, dear, we wouldn't go as far as that, wouldn't dream of it!" And run the risk of meeting Janice there too, perhaps, for you never know, she might still drop in at the Old George from time to time, maybe even hoping to meet up with Grace again. Grace did still sometimes wonder how Janice was managing — but not very often. Never look back had always been her motto. "We'll only be just round the corner."

"We'll be back before the news, Mother."

"Oh, very well. I can see there's no use arguing."

"All work and no play makes Jack a dull boy," said Grace, going out to put on her coat.

"Sitting in a saloon bar is not my idea of play," said Mrs. Robinson loftily, pressing the remote control button of the television and letting in a blast of sound.

"I'm sorry to 've upset your mother," said Grace as they walked up the road to where the buses breathed up and down Church Street. "I wouldn't do that for the world."

"She'll calm down." He was a bulky, tall figure beside her, in his dark clothes. "She's a great actress."

Grace was not sure how to take this. "I'm sure."

They turned the corner and started up the hill. After a while he said, "The thing is, you have to be firm. I've had to be firm to keep my independence. She's a wonderful woman but she likes to be centre stage all the time."

"I think you're wonderful with her. There's not many as have a son like you."

"Yes, well . . . She's used to being the star, you see. My father gave into her all along the line, worshipped the ground she walked on. A quiet sort of man, older than she was."

"She told me."

"His death upset her. She wasn't used to being on her own. While she was still in the theatre, of course, she was full of life, still felt in the centre of things. But later — well, she was getting older, there weren't the parts. . . . It seemed sensible to move in with her at the time."

"You were on your own too, were you?"

"At that time." His face shut down on the words and he said nothing more till they reached the public house.

The saloon bar was small, all ruby and plush, ruby lighting from small frilled shades, a durable carpet of diverse patterns on which stood small solid tables and solid benches with ruby cushions. It was no more than pleasantly full of people talking quietly over their drinks, Muzak and fruit machines confined to the public bar.

Grace loosened her jacket, removed her head scarf, looking round with satisfaction. This was just right, just the sort of respectable, cosy place to get him relaxed in, better than the Old George with its mixed West End crowd. When he came back with her gin and vermouth and his claret she smiled at him with genuine pleasure. "This is really nice."

During the next hour or so, in the warmth and subdued lighting and restrained to and fro of company, he did relax. His face grew rosier and slightly moist, his solid body leaned back and seemed to loosen, his eyes lost their defensiveness, and he talked. But he told her nothing she did not already know, gave her no clue as to those blanked-out years or that mysterious Wednesday. He talked about the news, the changing pattern of English weather, a little about his work. Desperate to draw him into more intimate subjects, Grace talked about herself — her whirlwind wartime romance, still hardly more than a child, her idyllic brief marriage, her husband's death soon after the war from a wound gained while crossing the Rhine; her brave fight to make a career for herself in nursing, her decision (wrong, perhaps, now) not to remarry, despite one or two offers. . . . "I like my independence, see, just as you do. But I sometimes wonder . . ." She gazed into her glass, "I mean, as one gets older . . ."

"I know what you mean," he said soberly, and she allowed a silence to grow between them before looking at her wristwatch (from that old girl in Putney back in the spring, and kept perfect time) and saying, "My word, we'd better be getting back! The time's just flown!"

He helped her on with her coat. As they left the pub she wondered if she should take his arm but decided not. Men were easily frightened. But she said with real warmth, "I really enjoyed that. It's just the sort of cosy place I like."

"Yes, it's a pleasant watering-hole." He took her elbow to cross into their own darker street but released it as usual almost at once.

"It makes a nice break, just to pop out to a place like that once in a while."

"Yes it does."

She could shake him!

She ventured, "Your mother's a wonderful woman but of course she's a bit demanding. Well, she would be, wouldn't she, being who she is. She's been used to having everything her own way. Old people get like that, it's understandable really." He agreed. They were halfway back to the flat. She decided to persist. "Of course, I've learned to put up with it — well, you don't get to SRN without learning that, I can tell you. But one does need a bit of a break sometimes, otherwise it all gets on top of you and you begin to wonder just how long you can go on."

This time he did react, and the expression she saw as they passed under a street light was alarmed.

"You're not thinking of leaving us?"

"Well no, not immediately, of course. I wouldn't dream of leaving you in the lurch. But I have to think of the future."

"Yes."

He said nothing more until they turned into the doorway of the block. He paused there, the caretaker's door to the right, the short passageway to his own flat ahead of them. He faced her, his expression earnest.

"I do sincerely trust," he said, "that you realise how much I appreciate your presence here. It's made all the difference to my life — Mother's too, of course." Grace murmured something modest. "I realise that you must have sacrificed a good deal to come to our rescue as you did. I don't know what I'd have done — she's a wonderful woman but

227

she's getting old and the thought of her being alone all day while I'm at business — well, it's been a great anxiety to me. And after her fall . . ."

"And you've got yourself to think of too, you mustn't forget that," Grace cooed. "You've got a right to a life of your own, especially in the years to come." She laid her hand on his arm just for a moment.

"Yes, there's that too. You can see it's not easy." He paused broodingly, then braced himself. "All I can say is I'm grateful beyond words for your stepping into the breach as you have, and I trust you realise it to the full."

"Oh I do, Conroy, I do. We'll just have to see how it goes, shan't we?"

"Yes." He sighed, and they walked in silence down the corridor to their front door.

For the truth of the matter was that Grace was getting browned off with the pair of them; she'd had enough of commodes and strip washing at the old folks' home, and Mrs. Robinson's queenly airs got up her nose. And she missed her independence, just like she'd said. She was prepared to put up with all this if it paid off, but after more than four weeks of it she was getting impatient.

She was not very good at long-term projects; she liked to plan schemes and then carry them out, no hang about while they matured. This was why the scheme with the old folks had been so satisfying — no hanging about, just find one, work it, and out. In many ways the set-up had been ideal, and Janice (no matter what her deficiencies) the ideal partner.

But if the Robinsons paid off, they would be the really big one. It had to be big otherwise it was simply a waste of time; and until she knew whether he was married or single she was stymied.

While Mrs. Robinson had her afternoon nap next day Grace nipped into Conroy's room and took the locked japanned box back into her own. There, using old skills and a variety of domestic implements, she at last clicked it open. Carefully, keeping everything in order, she examined its contents.

There were two building society books, each showing — whew! — between twenty-five and thirty thousand in deposits. There was his national service paybook; he had been in the Royal Engineers and reached the grade of sergeant. Tucked into this was a set of postcards showing an unlikely nun doing even more unlikely things to an improbable, birettaed priest; both protagonists looked distinctly Middle Eastern, and some of Conroy's service had been in Cyprus. There were insurance documents on the flat and contents, and letters concerned with one on his life, linked to his working pension, held by his office, so no details. Grace supposed the old girl would be the beneficiary. There was a photograph of the elderly man Grace now knew was his father; none of his mother — no need, since there were plenty of those about the flat anyway. There was a photograph of a girl with the high-rolled, blondied hair-do, the small waist and swirling skirts of the 1950s, leaning against a gate. There was a copy of Conroy's birth certificate, of his father's death certificate, of the Decree Absolute granted to Conroy Edward Robinson from Carole June Ann Robinson, née Palmer, 1976.

Ha! Got it!

There were other papers but Grace did not bother to look further. That absence of which his mother sourly refused to speak was when he married — out of the services, presumably, the marriage certificate perhaps destroyed in bitterness, only the tug of the past and the certainty of the present preserving the photo and the divorce certificate.

Grace put the documents carefully back into the box. Relocking it was a little difficult but she assumed Conroy seldom looked at these papers and would never notice that it was not quite clicked shut. She replaced it in the bottom of his wardrobe, gave a smooth to her neat hair in his mirror, went out and closed the door quietly behind her. Now she could proceed.

Marion Robinson was a woman of such invincible conceit that even the recognition of a mistake was converted into merit. After several weeks of Grace as housekeeper she could congratulate herself on her realisation that Grace was a mistake.

When Conroy had first asked if he might bring a friend to Sunday tea she had immediately refused. It would not be a man — Conroy had never had male friends, being far too reserved to be convivial — and she had at once feared the friend to be some predatory little floozy like that bitch Carole, who had bowled him over just after he came out of the army and married him even before he had shown her to his mother; he had known very well, no doubt, what short work Marion would have made of her. Off he had gone, to some poky little Fulham flat, building up his career with the building society, and visiting Marion only once a month or so and that without Carole, thank you, after the first few meetings. This had suited Marion quite well, in fact, for she was right in the thick of things theatrical then, a handsome actress of fairly wide range, a handsome woman still not averse to what the great Mrs. Pat (whom Marion tried to resemble) had described as "the hurly-burly of the chaise-longue," and she enjoyed the role of discarded mother, her only child stolen away by a worthless sex bomb.

The estrangement had lasted a long time; even after Carole had left him for someone else he had continued to live on his own, although his visits to Marion became more frequent, every weekend. Then the Salt and Pepper comedies had ended, Marion had only "Nanny Jane" to keep her going. Her looks and her style belonged to the past, her blood pressure went up and her legs hurt her. Friends died or grew old themselves or, still in the cut-throat camaraderie of the theatre, dropped her.

She got Conroy back.

But not quite back. His years away (and an inherited something of her own self-will) enabled him to elude total subjugation. He had grown into a big, solid man, head of a department, a good cook and housekeeper, self-sufficient. It had needed her attack of shingles and the glimpse it gave him of the dependence on outside support and admiration of a woman he had always thought was totally confident that had forced him back. Without an audience she would crumble into nothing, so he became that audience. But not a member of the cast.

She had enjoyed his ownership of a car and had liked to be driven out of London every weekend, to the sea or to a stately home, and had also shared his annual holiday with him, touring or, as she became less mobile, in some agreeable resort. After a few years of this he had sold the car, not telling her beforehand; to her indignant protestations he had simply said that local parking had become impossible and that in any case it was now so difficult for her to get into the car that there was no point in keeping it. She was outraged but powerless; powerless too when he arranged a fortnight's stay for her each September at a home for disabled in Folkestone — very comfortable, very well run and very expensive, she could never complain about that. He himself went off to Corfu, Madeira or the Lake District, sending her many postcards. On return she would get little out of him but told him, resentfully, every detail of her own static two weeks. She was powerless, too, about the two nights off a week that he had quietly instituted, Wednesdays and Sundays; complain, rage, sulk though she did, he simply went his way. At first she had feared it was a woman and taxed him with it. "I like to play bridge," he had replied calmly, "and I like to get out and observe the passing scene once in a while." After a time she accepted that this was the truth.

So when he had suggested inviting a Mrs. Black, a pick-up from a West End pub, she was both alarmed and wary, agreeing purely as a defensive move. The appearance of a middle-aged widow, neat and deferential, not quite a lady, was greatly reassuring. She had seemed quite overawed by her surroundings and by the eminence of her hostess, not at all familiar with Conroy, and certainly understanding disabilities and how to help one in and out of chairs and other matters, where so often would-be helpers merely tugged and shoved. She began quite to look forward to the woman's Wednesday visits, finding her useful not only as an errand person but as a captive audience, credulous and admiring.

Then came her fall. That shook her far more than just physically. What she would have done if Mrs. Black had not been there she shuddered to think, overdramatising her genuine fear in an attempt to minimise it. She could have lain there for hours, helpless, cold — wet, she briefly acknowledged with added terror. She could have broken a limb, lost consciousness from the agony. She could have struck her head on the washbasin and got a concussion. She could have died. Conroy could have returned home at last and found her dead.

Thank God the woman had been there and known what to do! She had coped so kindly and sensibly, got her up and into bed with professional skill, had soothed and ministered, had made no reference whatsoever to that shaming sodden skirt and knickers and far-spread pool on the bathroom floor, that ultimate humiliation. That weakness and the realisation that she was no longer invulnerable shook Marion Robinson to her deepest core — more than when Conroy sold the car, more than the death of her husband, more than when Coral Brown got all the leads that Marion had hoped for at Stratford-upon-Avon that inter-war season.

For the days following she clung to Conroy, demanding and imperious, keeping him home from his office, at her beck and call. She was terrified to be left alone in a flat which now seemed isolated, in which she could die unnoticed. When he told her Mrs. Black had agreed to move in with them for a week or two it was as though all the footlights had flooded up.

She had no intention of showing her relief. When Conroy told her she put on a sour face and said, "I don't much care for a stranger living in."

"She's not a stranger, Mother. We've known her for weeks."

"On a superficial basis. Oh, very well! At least she's a trained nurse."

But oh, the pleasure of not being alone all day! Of being deftly helped to wash and dress, of being brought coffee on a pretty tray rather than in the slopped mug of the weekly woman (who had so disgracefully decamped when asked to do a little extra, these people have no loyalty), of having someone to talk at, direct and make complete use of!

For a few weeks it had been perfect. Mrs. Black — Grace — had gone about her tasks with respectful efficiency. True, she would call Marion "dear," which was common, but kindly meant. True, she did tend to insinuate her own routines into those of the Robinsons, but that was inevitable when running a household. True, she had upstaged the doctor into talking to herself rather than to his patient, but as his instructions were for Mrs. Robinson's care, that was understandable. For a little while Marion preened herself on having got very much the best of the bargain. Grace seemed a treasure.

But was she? Had she in fact, after all, got her eye on Conroy?

Marion's suspicions had started when they

had gone to the local pub together that Sunday. Only for an hour, only just round the corner, but even so. . . . It was a change in Conroy's routine which she knew must have been instigated by Grace, for Conroy (as she knew only too well) was inflexible, left to himself. The years-old battle over his weekly two nights off still rankled but she had had to accept them, reconciled because she did not feel she was under personal threat; no other person was involved, he simply liked to play bridge (the Saturday games with the Lorings were not enough for him) and to sit (heaven knew why!) among noisy strangers in a West End bar. Well, *chacun à son goût*. He had always been a self-contained boy, never showing much emotion even on first nights when she had him backstage in her dressing-room amid the telegrams and kisses and bouquets. Which had made his capture and marriage to that bitch Carole all the more of a shock.

That was all a long time ago. Once he had returned to his mother, all that nonsense behind him, he had been the perfect son. His little flights of obstinacy and independence (although it was extremely selfish of him to get rid of the car, she had so much enjoyed their outings) could be indulged. His holidays alone — no, she could never forgive him those, even though she knew they would now have been too much for her. But they had done him no harm, he had returned to her exactly the same as when he had left, save for a touch of sunburn, and although she did complain she was confident she had no cause to.

In the first few minutes of meeting Mrs. Black, Marion's apprehension that she might be another Carole had been calmed. This neat, respectable middle-aged woman, with her chain-store two-piece and sensible shoes, her speech, which was that of the superior working-class, was the perfect housekeeper. A long-time widow with no desire to marry again (or she surely could have done so), of modest independent means, a trained nurse — who could be better to minister to Marion Robinson's needs, and she realised at once that this was what Conroy had in mind. At first a regular visitor, to run errands and to listen; then, after the fall, a lifeline.

So it had been, freeing him and satisfying her. The perfect manipulation of a compliant tool. How fortunate!

Until that Sunday hour or so at a local bar. It could not have been at Conroy's suggestion — indeed, he had probably been rather put out but too well mannered to refuse; anxious, too, not to offend his mother's menial. They had not been absent long but he had seemed ever so slightly flustered when they returned, while she, Grace, had clearly enjoyed herself. She had been as quietly spoken as usual, had bustled about and brought Mrs. Robinson her hot whisky and water as usual, had helped her to bed and given her feet a rub with eau de cologne and said good night, sleep tight (irritating, this, but must be tolerated). But there had been an air of satisfaction about her which Marion did not care for. Conroy had said nothing, had opened a bottle of claret and sat down in front of the television with it while Grace helped his mother to bed, uncommunicative as always. Despite her customary sleeping pill, Mrs. Robinson had uneasy dreams.

Thereafter she watched Grace closely. There was no discernible change in her manner; but was there just the slightest hint of familiarity when she spoke to Conroy, a slightly more intimate smile? Was she becoming just the slightest bit brusque in her manner to Mrs. Robinson?

Yes, she was. She was not always quite so quick to obey commands, to fetch this or adjust that. "Rightyoh, dear, hang on a tick," she would say and continue what she was doing, while Mrs. Robinson must endure the slipped cushion or the *Telegraph* out of reach (had Grace even read it herself first? — unthinkable!) or, most humiliating of all, the not-immediate trek to the lavatory. She was not always as patient as she had been with Mrs. Robinson's reminiscences: "Yes, dear, you've told me that before," and she would get up and go into the kitchen. Or she would dump Mrs. Robinson rather roughly on to her bed or yank her rather too hard under the armpits to get her settled against her pillows or leave her rather too long stuck on the lavatory seat, her knees getting cold. "Sorry, dear, I can't be everywhere at once," she would say, and follow Mrs. Robinson and her walking-frame too closely back down the passage so that she felt she must go faster, nervous of Grace's impatience.

She did not like being nervous; she was afraid if she felt nervous. She had never been nervous, even on first nights, confident of always being in control. Now she was nervous.

She tried to override it by being even more imperious. "Bring me a handkerchief," "This tea is far too strong," "Surely you know by now I never take mustard," dropping the please and thank you. Scowling in her chair, resentful at her physical dependence, she struggled for dominance, to assert her authority again over what, in those first weeks of acquaintance, had seemed the perfect, humble slave.

She suspected now that she had been mistaken. No, not mistaken (she did not make mistakes) — misled. Conroy's touching concern for her had led her to indulge his wish that she should have a companion. She had recognised at once, of course, that Grace was not a lady but of what seemed the superior domestic class, like a good cook-general or theatrical dresser (Jessie, who had looked after her all those years of Salt and Pepper had been just such a one). This had seemed an advantage, she would know her place. Then, after the fall, her place had changed; she had become essential, her moving in a godsend; for, deeply hidden, almost from herself, Marion was terrified of another fall, a stroke, a heart attack, dying alone, the ultimate failure of command. She had intended to make use of this respectful Mrs. Black to the full.

She had been misled. These people were all the same, out for what they could get. But what was it that Grace Black could get?

Conroy?

When Conroy was there Grace was all sweetness and light, attentive, self-effacing, the perfect housekeeper. Sometimes in the kitchen, preparing vegetables for one of his weekend cook-ups or washing-up while he meticulously dried, she would say good-humouredly, "Her ladyship was in a rare old paddy this morning. I couldn't do anything right." His face would go dull and she would laugh in an indulgent way and say, "I don't take no notice of it, not when she's like that. Old people is all the same, they all have their little ways." A day or so later she might say, not so light-heartedly, "Your mother was in a rare old mood today, nothing would please her. Made me feel like the cat brought in."

"You mustn't let her upset you."

"Oh, I don't, don't you worry. Old people have these moods, turn against their nearest and dearest very often. It's something to do with the blood not getting to the brain."

He polished a glass as though he were wringing his hands. "I know she can be difficult . . ."

"Well, she's entitled, isn't she, a grand old girl like her. I try not to take it personal." She squeezed out the mop, emptied the washing-up bowl with a great swirl of sudsy water and turned to him with a smile. "Never say die, eh?"

Presently he suggested they might go out to the Lamb for half an hour. Sunk in her chair in front of the nine o'clock news, Mrs. Robinson watched them go with hot eyes.

Although he still kept to his rule of going out after supper every Wednesday, not returning till midnight or so (as Grace in bed and smoking her rare cigarette, with her transister turned on low, stayed awake to confirm), he had given up going up west on Sundays and instead took Grace to the Lamb. Perhaps he did not want to offend her by going off on his own to what had been their original meeting place. Perhaps he really did prefer her company and the quiet surroundings so near to home. And once a week or so, if Grace had made one of her half-humorous complaints about his mother, he took her there on a weekday for what he called "a breather," one gin and vermouth for her, two glasses of claret only for him, hardly more than half an hour but enough to mollify, in his ponderous way, her not quite concealed dissatisfaction. He talked of this and that but always came round to his mother's eminence and his appreciation of Grace's presence. Grace had at first modestly disclaimed her own virtues (if one can't have a bit of understanding, she's a wonderful woman, we pass this way but once . . .) but as her impatience grew she began to insinuate doubts.

"I do feel sometimes just a bit at the end of my tether. Sometimes these days I don't seem to do anything right," turning the glass of gin and vermouth thoughtfully on the small table in front of them.

"She gets very frustrated, not being independent. She's always been so independent."

"I can see that."

"You mustn't feel it's anything personal. It's just she's always been used . . ."

"Yes, well, of course I know that. She's always been the queen bee, hasn't she, and it must come hard on her now. But I've not been used to not living my own life either. It's not very nice being spoken to like a servant when one's only trying to be kind."

"She gets carried away. The arthritis . . ."

"Perhaps she might be better off in a home, having treatment. They do ever such wonderful operations now, almost as good as new." He blenched, but she went on, "I don't know quite how long I can carry on sometimes, not if she's going to go down hill. It's the muddle, see, not knowing just who's really in charge. It's me as does all the running of the place, all the nursing and fetching and carrying and the responsibility when you're at business, but it's her who thinks she's still the boss and speaks to me sometimes like I was dirt."

His face had gone red while she spoke and now paled, a large square mask of appalled clay. His voice was hoarse. "You mustn't feel like that, Grace. It's just her way. We both of us know to the full just how much we depend on you."

244

"Oh I know *you* do, Conroy." She gave him a wistful smile. "And don't think I'm complaining. She's a wonderful woman and I'm only too glad I've been able to help out a little. But I do have my own life to lead."

He seemed to sink down inside himself, despair in every fleshy plane. "I don't know what we'd do without you."

"Oh, come along now, you'd soon learn to manage. After all, you'll be retired soon. You can get the district nurse and meals on wheels, and you could put her in a home if you wanted a break now and then."

"It'd kill her."

"Nonsense, dear. It might kill you but it wouldn't kill her," she laughed, and finished her drink. "Anyway it's not come to that yet, has it? Only it does get me down a bit sometimes, taking all that stick. It'd be easier if we was all quite clear as to who's in charge there, if I had some real authority. Like as if, you know, it was really my home."

Her words stayed in the silence between them, amid the clink of glasses and quiet chat, the muted Muzak from the public bar, the to and fro of the swing door. The subdued lighting focussing the dazzle of the bar, the warm air, pleasantly scented by liquor and cigarette smoke, made a cocoonlike atmosphere in which the two of them sat together at their table, stilled by the prospects of the future.

She let the silence lie; then, looking at her wristwatch, gave a start and a cheerful exclamation. "My goodness, look at the time! I'd better get back or her ladyship's going to have kittens!" She pulled her cardigan over her shoulders, gathered her handbag. "Don't you come, dear, there's no need, not if you'd like a bit longer on your own. I'll tell her you've gone for a walk."

She extricated herself from bench and table while he half-rose from his seat. He still looked awful.

"If you're sure . . ."

"Not to worry. You stay for a while, you don't often get much of a break. Cheerybye." With a smile and a wave she left the bar. The doors went slap-slap behind her.

For a few days Conroy did not suggest another visit to the Lamb. It might be that she had alarmed him into facing alternatives — that was a risk she had knowingly taken; or it might be that he was afraid to hear that her mind was further made up to leave them — which had been Grace's purpose. In that case, he must stew in his own juice for a while; and had he invited her she would have found some excuse not to go. It was a delicately balanced operation and Grace played it skilfully.

When Conroy was there she was all patience and self-effacement, leaving it to him to carry out many of his mother's commands with an air of understanding that of course he would wish to, these little services, duties . . . The more intimate duties she took from him with quiet authority, absolving him, with a smile and a cheery word, from such unpleasant necessities. "You sit and watch 'Panorama' dear, she'd say, I'll see to her," raising a glowering Mrs. Robinson from her chair with professional ease and disappearing down the passage towards the lavatory, the undressing, the bed; her own non-reappearance leaving him uneasily alone with the television, not knowing quite what rituals he was being spared, wondering if Grace had gone to her own room offended, upset, angry, disgruntled . . . ? Grace, in her dressing-gown, feet up on one of MARION CONROY's trunks, smoked her last cigarette of the day and listened to Capital Radio turned low, content.

But when Conroy was absent through the working day her attitude to Mrs. Robinson was decidedly sharper. She was not always as gentle as she might be getting her out of or on to anything; when Mrs. Robinson complained (as she did) Grace would say, "Well, you're getting heavier, you know, dear. It's only natural," or "Well, you don't try and help yourself, do you, dear. I can't heave up a dead weight, can I?" She smoked while working in the kitchen although Mrs. Robinson had, right from the beginning, stated she would not have smoking in the flat, and even sometimes came into the sitting-room with a cigarette in her mouth. When Mrs. Robinson furiously complained Grace said, "Sorry, dear, I forgot" and took her time returning to the kitchen where she might or might not stub it out. Mrs. Robinson's lunches became less interesting (although her supply of alcohol increased) and Grace said, "Well, dear, when you're chair-bound like you are you need plenty of roughage, nothing spicy, else you'll have trouble"; and sure enough, after Conroy's more tasty weekend meals she did have indigestion. The whisky, which Grace never stinted, eased that.

Grace now often came into Mrs. Robinson's bedroom without knocking, with a cheery "Sorry, dear, we need to get a move on." This was particularly infuriating to the old lady when, having managed to get herself to the dressing-table, she was putting on her make-up, something no one was ever allowed to watch. Astringent, moisturiser, foundation, all were carefully applied to the soft, hardly lined flesh that years of theatrical greasepaint and cold cream had preserved. Eye shadow, eyebrow pencil (hardly any natural hairs left, age depilitated one in most surprising places); rouge, powder, lipstick. Bustling in without knocking, Grace said indulgently, "I don't know why you take so much trouble, dear, there's no one here today but me," or "You've overdone it a bit today, dear, I expect you don't see so well." The itinerant hairdresser who visited Mrs. Robinson for years had been twice since Grace had come to live, and the old lady's hair had remained its metallic black. But as the next appointment approached Grace had begun to say things like "I don't know why you want to spend the money, dear. I can give you a shampoo and set as good as her and as for the tinting . . ." (Mrs. Robinson filled with rage, it was a taboo subject) ". . . why don't you let yourself go your natural grey, I always think tinting's so ageing."

"Is your own colour natural?" Mrs. Robinson demanded, her face red with fury.

"Yes," Grace answered blandly, and went out of the room.

It was difficult for Mrs. Robinson to put any of this into precise words when she and Conroy were alone — which was not often. Although when she complained, Conroy said little, his face, his whole body, became more squarely set, a solid block of obduracy; he did not want to hear.

"She's dreadfully familiar, Conroy, she speaks to me sometimes as though I were a half-wit."

"I'm sure you're imagining, Mother."

"No, I am not! She even went out of the room while I was speaking to her this morning, right in the middle of what I was saying."

Her complaints sounded trivial, she knew. She could not bring herself to tell the more humiliating incidents, the roughness, the disregard of privacy, the wounding truths, for these would reveal her loss of power, the seeping away into the morass of old age of that dominance by which she had ruled her life and the lives of those near her. She could not admit, least of all to the son she had always commanded, that she was no longer supreme. "You must speak to her, Conroy," she ordered.

He did not reply at once but sat opposite her, square and solid in his chair, his square solid face expressionless. Then, "I can't," he said.

"Can't? What d'you mean, can't? She's our employee, isn't she?"

"That's it." He paused again, then looked at her straight. "She might leave."

For a moment she was taken aback. "So much the better. I don't have to put up with insolence in my own house."

"Mother." He set his hands one on either

250

arm rest and stared at her. "We have to have someone."

"Then find someone. There are plenty of women who would be glad to find such a good place."

"No, there are not. We know that already. You know how hard it was to find even Mrs. Walters and you always said she was no good. And before that, the home helps, remember? Never knowing whether they were coming or not, turning up at all hours, wouldn't do that, wouldn't do this. Only one of them was any good and she was moved on just when you'd got used to her. Do you really want to go back to that?"

"Of course not! But there must be retired trained domestics. You could advertise in the *Lady*, somewhere like that . . ."

"In any case," his voice overrode hers, "a daily won't do, not now. She would have to live in. You can't be on your own all day, not now."

She shrank back a little in her chair. Before her fall her head would have been level with the top of its padded back; now it was well below, sunk down nearer her hunched shoulders. "A good daily woman . . ."

"No, Mother. There's nights too."

She drew herself upright again with a return of her old spirit. "You want to keep her! She's got round you! It doesn't matter to you that I can't stand the woman, she's got round you!"

"Oh, Mother . . . !"

"Yes she has. I could see it coming. When you first brought her to tea that afternoon I could see she was after something. I could see she didn't know the least thing about the theatre, that class never do. I never trusted her, not for a moment." Her face had gone red and she was clutching the arms of the chair as though she would spring out of it and at him if she could.

"Mother. I brought her because I thought she might be useful to you, a friend."

"Friend!"

"Companion, then. And you liked her at first, you know you did. She did all sorts of little things for you, she *was* useful."

"Useful to you, you mean! You thought she'd let you out of your responsibilities, the little services you ought to be doing yourself. I know duty's a dirty word nowadays but it does exist!"

His face seemed to shift and quiver, half exasperation, half fear. "Mother, don't say such things."

"Why not? You're trying to shift me off on to this woman so that you can have more time to go off and do heaven knows what on your own! You don't care a ha'penny piece whether

I'm happy or not, as happy as I can be tied to this dreary flat day after day!" She seemed to swell, vigour flooding into her as the drama got into its stride. "You brought this woman into the house with the deliberate intention of shelving responsibilities, setting her above me in my own house, a common woman like that!"

"Hush — she'll hear you!"

"I don't care if the whole street hears me! She's wound you round her little finger and you're too soft to see it."

He got to his feet and stood over her as though his sheer bulk could muffle her words. "Mother, if she hears she'll leave. Now, immediately. We'll be left with no help of any kind, not domestic, not nursing. I can't help you to the toilet, washing, undressing — it's not fitting. We have to have her, Mother, things aren't the same since you had your fall."

They stared at one another, and Marion felt a great wave of despair flood up through her body, bearing tears ahead of it, bitter and held back with desperate pride. Rage had always been her way, rage and arrogance and often cruelty, never tears. Never even counterfeit weakness, but always strength. Now, sunk in her chair with the painful useless legs of her old age, counterfeit strength.

"Very well," she said after a while, "I see

that it's convenient to keep her for the time being. But I want you to look for a replacement, Conroy. At once. The *Nursing Times,* that might be the place. Do you hear me?"

"Yes."

"And I'd prefer it if you didn't hobnob with her in pubs any more. She should know her place."

The tension had gone out of him and he turned away, finding and opening the *Radio Times* in the hope of getting things back to normal. But he said, "I can't just stop. She'd think it odd. We don't want to offend her."

"*You* don't want to offend her." The façade of her authority was in place again. "Very well. But I have your promise, haven't I?"

He said nothing but moved towards the television set. "I should like a small whisky, if it wouldn't be too much trouble."

"Marion's got her knife into Mrs. Danvers, I see," said Dickie Loring as they drove home after bridge that Saturday. "I thought the honeymoon wouldn't last."

"Poor woman, I don't envy her," Wendy said comfortably.

"I suppose she knew what she was doing. I'd say she'd been around."

"She seems a nice woman. And poor old Marion has to have someone now — hasn't she gone down hill all of a sudden? So sad."

"I bet poor Conroy's wetting his pants she'll leave."

They lived nearby in one of the few remaining rent-restricted flats behind Westbourne Grove, and soon turned into their road. Unclicking her seat belt from her bundled coverings, Wendy said, "D'you think we ought to warn her?"

"Marion?"

"No, Mrs. Black. I mean, it is her home now, darling, and she may not realise she could be out on her ear. Marion can be such a bitch." It was raining and she put a plastic hood over her white curls before getting out of the car and scuttling up to the portico. Dickie checked that the car doors were locked, then followed her.

"We might. Best play it by ear." They let themselves in, went up the stairs, opened their own front door. The flat was warm. He put his arm round her and gave her a kiss. They were still fond of one another.

After the scene with his mother Conroy let a Sunday go by without inviting Grace to join him at the Lamb. He had gone out himself and up to the Old George but said nothing, and neither his mother nor Grace enquired. As he left, Mrs. Robinson had sent a glance of triumph to where Grace sat looking through the *Sunday Telegraph* magazine, and called sweetly to her son, "Don't hurry back, dear, I shall be quite all right." The two women had watched television almost without speaking until it was the old lady's bedtime, Mrs. Robinson plump with satisfaction, Grace serene. The undressing, toilet, settling, were performed without friction. Each, in due course, slept.

Nothing was said. Mrs. Robinson did not ask him if he had advertised as she had wished; she was sure that he had but not so sure as to risk enquiry. But his obedience in not inviting Grace restored her confidence and her imperious ways were almost benign. She relived for Grace many of her theatrical successes, with anecdotes of the famous of whom Grace had never heard, calling for her books of press cuttings, her heavy albums of photographs, her cardboard boxes of fake jewellery, even the dragging out from under its covers in Grace's bedroom the big trunk in which, layered in plastic, tissue and moth repellant, were stored the more precious of her stage costumes — a cloak, a crown, some of the grand evening dresses of her Salt and Pepper dowager days.

Grace had seen them all before, had heard the anecdotes many times. With her pleasant smile she let it all roll over her, not listening, knowing only that this puffed and sunken body, these big-veined discoloured hands, those swollen legs, the whole decaying carcass of this old cow would sit there in her own mess if Grace were not there to heave her up and lug her to the toilet and come when she called, like as if she was a servant. At least in the old folks' home they had known who was boss.

So she too said nothing but was remote and gentle in the kitchen with Conroy where, for a few days, he took care not to be too often, afraid of reproach. But she showed none, only an understanding reticence that gradually re-assured him. He went out as always on the Wednesday, the Lorings came to bridge as usual on Saturday (giving Grace some sym-pathetic looks at Marion's sharper orders be-fore Grace left them to their game, and Dickie pressing her hand more meaningfully than usual when she emerged to see them out); but on the second Sunday Conroy invited her. With quiet dignity she accepted.

He was more than usually silent, even for him. She did not intrude, save now and then with a bland comment on the weather or the less disturbing news of the day. She sipped, observing the other customers; he drank, mo-rose and ill at ease. The silences lay between

257

them, serene on her side, wary on his. At length, as they got up to go, he said, "Everything all right, is it?"

She smiled, adjusting her scarf. "Well — never say die. We'll survive."

He followed her out into the street. "She's been all right, has she?"

She allowed a pause to lengthen before replying. "She's ever so wilful. Old folk get like that, like children. Only I haven't the authority, see, not like with children. If I had the authority, officially like . . ." Her words drifted away, leaving their implications in the air between them.

As they reached the apartment building and he got out the keys she put her hand on his arm. In the dingy light above the entry porch her face looked concerned and comely. "Don't you fret," she said, "I wouldn't leave you in the lurch, not without warning." He blenched. She gave his arm a pat. "Never say die, eh?" She took the keys from him, opened the door and went in. Dumbly he followed her.

Nothing was said. Conroy kissed his mother good night and shut himself in his room. In silence Mrs. Robinson — a volcano from which only a glare, a wisp of smoke, gave sign of the turbulence within — allowed Grace to heave, support, unzip, fetch, carry, commode, nightcap with the half-tumbler of whisky and water that had become a ritual, arrange pillows, drop down on to bed, lift gnarled feet with their yellowing toenails and hide them under the bedclothes, tuck, pat, smile.

"Shall I take your dentures, dear?" Mrs. Robinson's lips clamped shut. "Rightyoh then, but don't forget and leave them in. You don't want sore gums, do you?"

She switched off the main light. In the side shadows of the bedside lamp Mrs. Robinson's bulk looked like some huge, half-disintegrated bust, shawled and hair-netted.

"Sleep tight, then, sweet dreams."

She shut the door, saw Conroy's light was out from the gap under his door, went quietly down the passage to the lounge and there, in Mrs. Robinson's chair and her feet up on the hassock looked through next week's *TV Times* and smoked the last cigarette of the day.

Next morning things were as usual. Grace gave Conroy his breakfast, saw him off to business with her usual, "Have a good day"; took Mrs. Robinson hers on a tray; had her own with the *Daily Telegraph* — not too careful to refold it exactly for Mrs. Robinson, who liked to read it in pristine condition when she was dressed and settled in her chair later on. She washed up, tidied her room, ran the Hoover over the lounge. Mrs. Robinson liked to be up, helped wash and dress and left on her own to put on her warpaint before that was done, but it now suited Grace better to do it first, and lately that was what she had been doing. It meant the old girl had to wait for the toilet, which sometimes led to accidents; but that was no bad thing.

Nothing was said, save an occasional order and Grace's platitudes. Mrs. Robinson achieved her chair, noted the crumpled pages of the *Telegraph,* drank her elevenses. Grace popped out to the shops, saw what was on at the local cinema, had a coffee among the plastic vineleaves of Perugini's Café-Ristorante. She fancied going down to Kensington High Street, for it was a nice day; but there was the old girl's lunch to see to and her own, she might pop down afterwards.

She did fish fingers and some mash for lunch, with fruit yoghurt to follow. They ate at the table in the french windows looking out over the small yard which, as autumn neared, did not get the sun till later. A few roses still flowered on the trellis up the whitewashed wall but the shrubs in the earthenware pots had gone only to leaf. Mrs. Robinson would have liked her lunch brought to her on a trolley and Grace to have hers in the kitchen. Grace would have liked them both to eat in the kitchen; it was far more practical even if it did mean lugging the old girl there. But no, it had to be the lounge, with the table properly set and the "World at One" on the radio. Mrs. Robinson took coffee afterwards, insisting it should be freshly ground; so it had been in the first weeks, but now Grace couldn't be bothered and merely made Nescaff very strong and gave her that — she'd never noticed the difference.

Grace liked to listen to "The Archers" after that; but the old girl couldn't stand them, unable to forgive them their longevity while Nanny Jane had been killed off long ago. So Grace used to hustle her to her afternoon lay-down and have "The Archers" on her own during the washing-up.

But not today. Today when she went to help Mrs. Robinson to her feet after the meal the old thing said, "I shall sit in my chair."

"Nonsense, dear, you need your bit of a zizz."

"I can have my "bit of a zizz,' as you call it, in my chair. I don't wish to go to my room." She was firmly attached to her walking-frame and pushed it past Grace with determination; shrunk though she was, she was still quite a formidable bulk. Grace stood back.

"Well, if that's what you want. Don't blame me if you're all stiffened up later."

She did not answer but reached her chair,

manoeuvred round, dropped into it with a thump. Grace did not help her but began to clear the table. Apart from the sounds of this, the silence grew as heavy as Mrs. Robinson's glare at Grace's busy figure. At last she said, "I know what you're up to, you know."

Grace hardly paused. "Oh? What's that, then?"

"You're after Conroy."

Now the silence really was heavy as Grace continued to scrape and stack the plates and add them to the tray. Then she turned to face Mrs. Robinson coolly.

"What makes you think that, dear?"

"It's perfectly obvious. I'm not a fool." Silence. "You won't succeed, you know."

"Oh? Want to bet?" She turned away and finished stacking the tray.

"Conroy is my son."

"And a pretty rotten life you lead him, too. A grown man tied to his mum."

Mrs. Robinson's face grew dark, her hands knotted on the arms of her chair. "Conroy's life is his own choice. He has his career, his bridge, he's free to do exactly as he wishes. That he's devoted to his mother is entirely natural."

Grace took the tray and went out of the room. In a moment she returned and began to remove and fold the tablecloth. Her face was bland, her eyes cold as glass.

Mrs. Robinson burst out, "He's had a full life, you know — he was in the forces and then he married. You didn't know that, did you?"

"Yes I did. She run out on him, didn't she?"

The old lady was shaken. "How do you know? He'd never speak of it."

"No?" She finished folding the cloth, smoothed it, put it in the drawer of the sideboard along with the table napkins.

Mrs. Robinson rallied. "It was a disaster, an utter disaster. He came back to me utterly shattered. I can assure you, Mrs. Black, that nothing and nobody could persuade him to marry again. Nothing!"

She sat glaring, her face red, breathing loud. Grace regarded her for a moment, then coolly came and sat down opposite in what was Conroy's chair. She crossed her legs and felt in the pocket of her apron for a cigarette packet, extracting one and lighting it slowly with her lighter, then sitting back and blowing a feather of smoke upward.

"What makes you think I'm interested in marriage?" she asked.

"What else? What else is a woman like you after?"

"Perhaps I'm what they call a caring person." Mrs. Robinson snorted. "Perhaps I just like looking after people, making them happy."

"Balls!"

"That's not a very nice expression, dear. I don't think Conroy'd like to hear his mother say a thing like that. But I suppose theatrical people are a bit racy."

"Conroy will never marry again!"

"I don't blame him. Marriage isn't so hot." She blew more cigarette smoke towards the ceiling, noting Mrs. Robinson's fury. "I've never been interested in sex, dear, it's only the legal side of things that are more convenient if you're married. Like property and insurance and who gets what in case of death. Marriage makes everything cut and dried, doesn't it, who has the actual rights."

"This flat is in my name."

"Yes, dear. But suppose you weren't responsible?"

"What do you mean?"

"Suppose you were in a home?"

The silence was full of shock. Then, "Conroy would never put me in a home."

"Wouldn't he? If there was no one here to see to you I reckon he'd have to."

Panic shrank Mrs. Robinson back into her chair, rage made her breath short. "We could find someone else. You're not irreplaceable."

"That's right, I'm not. You could try for a nurse, fifty pounds a day, and more, I daresay, when the time comes you need one at night time too. Or you could try for the Social Services — Attendance I think they call it, pop in and out when it suits them, a different one each time, I shouldn't wonder, maybe a darkie. Course, they've got all sorts of aids now — sheepskins so you don't get bedsores, pads for incontinence just like you was a great big baby. Or you could take a chance and advertise in a newsagents or somewhere and hope you didn't end up with a con man or worse." The ash fell from her cigarette on to the carpet.

After a moment Mrs. Robinson said, "Conroy will be retiring soon. We could certainly manage till then."

"I daresay you could. You've not gone down hill all that fast. But I don't see him wanting to spend his retirement years nursing his bedridden old mum."

"I'm not bedridden!"

"No, dear, not yet. Touch wood." She touched wood.

"You are a wicked woman," said Mrs. Robinson quietly. Colour had left her large face and her lipsticked mouth was garish against its greyness and the jetty hair. "You are trying to frighten me. I am not bedridden and my son would never put me in a home."

"Let's hope you're right, dear. I'm only trying to face facts. All I'm saying is I don't think Conroy would want to go it alone if I was to leave. He's got used to me being here and you have to admit I've taken a lot of the burden off him, poor chap. And I don't think he'd like giving up the rest of his life to nursing an old person — well, men don't, do they? I think when he leaves business he wants to live a little, travel around, relax. It's only natural. Now with me here . . ." She drew a long drag on her cigarette and looked about for an ashtray. There was none, so she rose and stubbed it out in the fireplace, leaving the squashed butt in the hearth and standing looking down on the old woman at bay within the arms and back of the chair, the metal fence of the Zimmer. "With me here that's just what he can do. His mind's at rest. He knows you're in good hands and he don't have to worry about a thing. We understand each other. I don't think he'd be willing to give all that up just because you've taken against me all of a sudden. Old people get funny like that, it don't bother me none. But of course" — she moved away and towards the door — "what does bother me a bit is my own position. I mean, how does it look to outsiders? Housekeeper's a bit of a funny description, isn't it? A bit like 'actress,' 'described as an actress,' the papers used to say and you knew what it meant all right. And then there's the business side of it — the bills and that and who decides when to redecorate or get new curtains. It puts me in a bit of a funny position, long term, and Conroy's aware of it. I've always valued my independence and that I've told him, but after all, one has to think of oneself sometimes, doesn't one, and there comes a time when maybe it's best to do things legal."

She opened the door and smiled cheerily.

"Well, all this talking won't buy the baby new shoes. I'd best get on with things."

She went out and shut the door. After the washing-up she took herself out and down to Kensington High Street as she'd planned, browsing the shops and giving herself a nice tea. She took care to be home before Conroy, and found Mrs. Robinson grey-faced on her bed. After hearing Grace go out, she had managed to get herself and her Zimmer to the lavatory but not quite in time; her knickers had suffered, but she had not the strength to do more than reach her bed and drop herself upon it, to lie, conscious of the smell, in a daze of terror and frustration. That evening she did not speak to Grace and hardly at all to Conroy; he sighed, meeting Grace's sympathetic glance, and thanked God for television.

Once Grace had started on a ploy she didn't hang about. She herself, in the most tactful way, initiated the following Sunday's visit to the Lamb and was especially womanly, drawing him out as best she could (no easy matter even now) about his job, his colleagues, his prospects for the future and retirement. "Retirement . . ." She let the word hang between them, seeming by her very reticence to give it a menacing quality. "Some people find it quite a shock. All that leisure suddenly and loss of authority. Twenty-four hours a day to fill, it makes you think. And I expect they miss the company, all the staff and companionship and that. I suppose it can be ever so lonely, till one's used to it." She took a sip. "Ah well," she said, "I'm sure you'll soon find something to occupy the time. And you've got your mother."

She left it there, and so did he: but she was confident his thoughts were moving in the right direction. She would get rid of those heavy velvet curtains to begin with; cleaned, they would fetch quite a few pounds in the right market, and she'd have something bright and cheerful in their place. And on the walls too, not that shabby old 1950s stuff and all those theatrical photos. And she'd have her room done up proper, not left like a boxroom; she didn't intend to move in with Conroy, thanks very much, and didn't think he would expect it. Although, once it was legal, if he insisted now and again she'd put up with it if she had to. But she didn't expect she'd have to. Conroy had never been a proper man — his wife running off and his mum draining away whatever get-up-and-go he might have had. Some men are like that, neutered toms . . .

With these satisfactory thoughts tucked away at the back of her mind, she ran into the Lorings outside Derry & Toms an afternoon or so later. They greeted her with a great show of delight and whisked her into a Viennese-style coffee shop, sweet with the smell of beverages and real cream gateaux. Side by side on the banquette Grace took off her head scarf and undid her mac while Wendy emerged from her nylon angora cardigan like a mouse from its nest. Opposite, dapper in a mock suede car coat, Dickie signalled grandly for a waitress.

"Isn't this *nice!*" cried Wendy in her childlike voice. "We've so often wanted to talk to you but we never get the chance. How *are* you, Grace?"

Grace, who had not known they were on

Christian name terms, smiled, patted her hair. "Mustn't grumble."

"How are *things?*"

Grace gave her a sharp look, saw only concern on the soft, elderly face with the oddly youthful eyes. She shrugged deprecatingly. "I take each day as it comes."

"We've *wondered,*" pursued Wendy. "You do seem to be quite wonderfully *relaxed.*"

His orders given, Dickie gave her his full attention. "We've known Marion for years. Wonderful woman. Good actress too, in her day."

"Too ham now, of course, even for radio. Can you imagine her in an RSC ensemble?" They giggled together.

"But seriously, Grace," Dickie said, "how's it going? We thought she was giving you rather a rough time."

Grace looked down, then up again with a smile. "I'm used to old folk. They've got a lot to put up with, poor old dears. We have to be patient."

"I'm sure you're patience itself." Dickie picked some brown coffee crystals from their dish and crunched them between dazzling dentures. "We've known Marion for years — I was in the box office all through the Salt and Pepper runs when Wendy first hove in sight."

"Goodness!" said Wendy, "I played that flirty schoolgirl! That's a hundred years ago, don't let's talk about it!"

The coffees came and they chose cakes.

Dickie crunched some more crystals. "Marion and Wendy met up again in the BBC Rep. They both did a stint with 'Nanny Jane.'"

"Happy days!" sighed Wendy, "Lovely regular money!"

"Sweetie-pie," said Dickie, "never look back." He broke the back of his Black Forest.

"But honestly, Grace love, we have *worried* about you. I mean, we know she doesn't mean it but she is rather hard to take sometimes and we have *wondered* if you could weather it all? They'd be absolutely sunk without you."

Grace looked embarrassed and sipped her coffee. It was not necessary for her to say anything, for the Lorings were saying it all.

"Marion's always been a *grande dame* and people simply won't put up with it now," said Dickie. "We've seen them come and go, haven't we, Wen — home helps, treasures, students earning some bread. She puts the backs up all of them."

"It's Conroy we're so sorry for, Grace. The poor darling's so wonderful with her."

"But what a life, eh? Can hardly call his soul his own."

"He should have broken away years ago,"

271

sighed Wendy, watching that her éclair cream should not shoot off the plate.

Grace, conservative with a Danish pastry, said carefully, "She did tell me he married."

"My *dear!*" Wendy gulped. "Indeed he did. Utter disaster!"

Dickie said judicially, "I don't think that was really Marion's fault, sweetie-pie. I mean, there was the most god-awful row when he broke the news, and I don't think they communicated at all till Carole ran off with that Australian and left him. And he didn't go home to Mum for quite a while after that, not till Nanny Jane ended and she was rather bereft."

"And now, poor darling, he's stuck. Until you came along, Grace. That's why we do so hope you'll put up with her and stay. He does so desperately deserve a bit of freedom."

Grace thought carefully before she said, "I did wonder if he might marry again."

Dickie drained his coffee cup. "Not a chance, darling. He's absolutely devoted to his Rosemary and of course she's R.C."

Wires thrummed, lights whirled. Grace felt as though all her blood was rushing down to her feet and up again in a thundering tide. When it receded, Dickie was ordering more coffee.

"It's absolutely hush-hush, Grace," said

Wendy earnestly, "Marion hasn't a clue."

"Best kept secret since D-Day," crunched Dickie.

"It's really rather sweet. I mean, he can only see her on Wednesdays because of her children — not that they're children any more, of course, but they're there every weekend and terribly demanding, rushing home from college or wherever with their laundry and so on and sort of acting like spies for their father. He's R.C. too, you see, even though he's left her, so it's all quite, quite hopeless."

"Marion'd have a fit if she knew. Carole was hard enough for her to take but Rosemary'd be even worse. Hence the bridge club cover."

"Poor darling Conroy, it's so horrid for him to have to lie and deceive her all this time — how long has it been, Dickie, four years, five?"

"Five, must be. It's four since he spilled the beans about it to us, he was pretty desperate then, in the first flush, you know, and had to unburden. Poor devil."

"So there they are, Grace, absolutely stuck and truly devoted. He's terribly sweet about her, isn't he, Dickie, all starry-eyed and steadfast. But with you there, and if only you'll stay, they might, just might manage to be together a little bit more. Her children aren't there during the week, you see, Grace, but then, of course, he's had to be with Marion, especially now when she's got so disabled. If you weren't there . . . You're an absolute godsend!"

"Bloody marvellous — tower of strength."

Wendy put her small paw on Grace's arm and gazed into her face. "That's why we've been so anxious, Grace. I mean, not only for you, the way Marion treats you sometimes, but for poor darling Conroy. Everyone deserves a little happiness in their lives, don't you think?"

Grace managed at last to speak. "What is this — Rosemary — like?"

"As a matter of fact," said Dickie, leaning back and smiling his ardent dental smile, "she's very like you."

Part Three

9

It was almost five weeks now, since the old lady's Suspicious Death. The usual catalogue of robberies, assaults, overdoses and rapes had filled Simpson's working hours, but he had not forgotten Miss Sybil Frimwell. Although he had never seen her — not even her corpse — her presence had seemed very strong to him as he had sat alone in her neat room, too bare of the objects that a human being collects over the years, the armchair beside the table (which so oddly had nothing on it, no cup, no pills) seeming to contain still the small light frame, the bright though faded eyes of an old woman who had been quite alone, no next of kin, had nothing but her own will to continue living, to retain her dignity and her privacy. Mr. Sobieski had described and respected her; the hospital staff where she worked, also. Even Leslie Pickering, nervously disclaiming all knowledge of her, had confirmed her qualities.

Photographs among her sparse papers had shown a small, thin child, a small, thin woman, each with a lively, even mischievous look to her, a look that was eager and enquiring. The photographs ended with a hospital group, all in white coats, a celebration of some kind. Dave had picked out Miss Frimwell, tiny among the others, by that same eager look, although by then (the 1960s would it be?) she was an elderly woman, the once bountiful hair thinner and gray: a small, wiry, determined person still involved with life. Not one to take an overdose. Not one even to have such pills prescribed.

He had not forgotten her. The case was not closed. At the back of his mind, she waited.

He was catching up on routine paperwork one mid-October afternoon when Leslie Pickering came to see him. There had been nobody's fingerprints on Pickering's carriage clock but his own, and with great reluctance Blane had returned it to him, after an overlong interval, still suspicious that Pickering could be their man. Blane was not the type to relinquish an idea easily; a crime was committed and someone had done it, and he could not adjust himself to the fact that crime and perpetrator did not go tidily two by two into the Law's ark. He did not forgive Simpson for the clock proving not to have been stolen from Miss Frimwell, and the case was not discussed between them.

Now Pickering was sitting tensely in one of the interview rooms, a car coat with a tartan lining thrown open, a Lenin-style cap crushed between his hands. His bald head shone, his eyes popped as Simpson entered; he half-rose, sank back, gasped a greeting.

Simpson sat across from him. "What can I do for you, sir?" He was surprised, intrigued, but did not show it, putting on his open, friendly face, the good-buddy, helpful-public-servant face.

Pickering inched his chair nearer, leaning towards Simpson over the table, still crushing his cap between his knees. "I've thought of something. It's probably nothing and I'm wasting your time, but I thought anything might be useful."

"In the matter of Miss Frimwell?"

"That's right. I know it's a long time ago and it's probably nothing. But it preys on my mind, you know, I can't forget it. And that other officer, I keep seeing him."

"D.C. Blane?"

"I don't know his name. That other officer who was with you. I keep seeing him."

"How d'you mean, sir?"

"It's probably nothing, all imagination. But I'm terribly sensitive, a death in the house, it really upset me, and then the police and all the questions. I was terribly upset when you took my clock. I couldn't sleep."

"I hope it's working O.K., sir? We kept it wound."

"Oh yes, yes, it's quite all right. It loses a little but it always did. It's just I couldn't think why you should think — I mean, why *my* clock? It upset me terribly."

"I'm sorry about that, sir." He was certainly in a state, almost in tears, pinker than ever, and the cap in his hands would never be the same. Could it be that, after all . . . ? But the clock had been clean, no one's dabs on it but his own. Hundreds of people owned carriage clocks, but it had seemed a coincidence worth checking out. Blane had been disappointed, for he'd taken against this poor little bugger with his twittering and his dolls. Nothing illegal in dolls.

He smiled his good-buddy smile. "But you've thought of something new, have you?"

"Yes. Yes I think so. It was seeing that other officer, you see, the light, the angle — I suddenly remembered. At least, I think I do, but it may be nothing."

"If you'd just tell me, sir."

"And he was so hostile. When he returned my clock he practically insisted on coming up, and he looked round again at all my

280

things and seemed to imply . . . I know I'm sensitive but it upset me terribly."

"Are you making a complaint, sir?" Simpson was suddenly grave, wary behind the official words. What the fuck had Blane been up to?

Pickering blenched. "No, no, nothing like that, I'm sure he was only doing his job. I quite understand. But it did upset me, and then seeing him outside the house several times, near my place of business and once near a — a club I go to sometimes . . ."

Simpson would have Blane's balls for this! Harassment. Christ! He said, "I'm sure those occasions were coincidences, sir. After all, it's D.C. Blane's manor, he's likely to be seen about the area quite a bit, nothing unusual in that, sir."

"No, no, I'm sure there isn't. I'm sure I'm imagining things. But he seemed so hostile when he called, as though he thought . . . And then when I saw him coming out of the gate yesterday I suddenly remembered . . ."

"What, sir?"

"He didn't see me, thank goodness. I suppose he'd intended to interview me again, although I'm sure I don't know what could have been the reason this time. I hung back when I saw him and he shut the gate and

281

went off up the road in the other direction. And although I was terribly upset, I suddenly remembered."

"Yes?"

"That day, early closing day — you think poor Miss Frimwell must have died on that Thursday, don't you?"

"We believe so."

"Well, as I was coming home that day, I was about five or six houses away, about half-past three, four o'clock it would have been because I stopped for lunch after the shop closed and then . . ." He flushed, crushing the cap between his hands. "I went to a sauna I sometimes frequent, I find it relaxes me, irons out the tensions . . ." Simpson nodded. He knew Pickering's movements on that Thursday, they had been checked by Blane early on. "And as I was coming along I remember now — at least, I think I do — two women came out of the gate and went off the same way the officer went."

"Away from you?"

"That's right."

"You didn't see their faces?"

"No, just their backs. I didn't think anything of it, wasn't even sure they came from my house, next door perhaps, I really wasn't noticing. But seeing your officer yesterday, something about the light and the angle and everything, I suddenly remembered. I'm sure it was from our house." He gazed at Simpson, plump and trusting.

"Let me get this straight. Between 3:30 and 4 P.M. on the day we believe this lady died, as you were approaching your house, you observed two women leaving the premises . . ."

"Not the premises, just the garden. They came out of the garden and closed the gate and walked away up the road."

"Right, sir. Leaving the garden. You don't know whether they had been in the house or not?" Pickering shook his head, leaning back now and laying the mangled cap on the table. "Can you describe the women?"

"One was tall, about your height. I think she had brownish hair, straight, down to her shoulders. The other was shorter, she had a scarf on her head. Broader. I'd say she was older."

"Clothes?"

"Oh dear, I can't be sure. I wasn't really noticing, you see, why should I? I was just vaguely aware of two women walking away up the street."

"Just the same, try."

Pickering shut his eyes for a moment, his round face clenched in concentration.

"I think the taller one wore jeans, trousers of some sort. The other I couldn't say — a skirt and jacket perhaps? And the scarf, I noticed the scarf, only older women seem to wear them now. Like the Queen."

"Colour?"

"The scarf? Some sort of pattern, I think, pink and blue perhaps. Perhaps a navy jacket, dark anyway. The taller one I simply don't recall, I'm so sorry . . ."

"Not to worry. You've been very helpful. The only thing is, sir, I wonder why you've left it so long?"

Anxiety almost thinned Pickering's face. "It was your officer — when he brought back my clock. He implied — he seemed to think there was something sinister about it and that in some way I . . . As though there'd been a *crime.*"

He would castrate Blane! "There are certain discrepancies."

"He seemed to imply there was something not quite right about Miss Frimwell's death. That somehow I had something to do with it and that you would have to interrogate me again. It upset me terribly. I mean, I hardly knew Miss Frimwell, I knew nothing about her. I told him, I hardly ever spoke to her, I wasn't even in the house when you think she died. And he looked at me in a really nasty way and said something like I'd better try and remember anything

I could as the police didn't like people with-holding information."

Simpson said carefully, "D.C. Blane is a very conscientious officer, sir. I'm sorry if he upset you, he does have a somewhat unfortunate manner at times but it's all in the cause of doing his job. And in fact, sir," he gave his good-buddy smile again, "he has jogged your memory, hasn't he?"

"Well yes — yes, I suppose he has. It made me think and think about that afternoon, and then when I saw him coming out of the gate and walking away it came back at me — I mean that I had seen two women doing just what he had done, and at the same time of day. And I was so glad he hadn't seen me and that I hadn't been in, because I really do find him very upsetting. So I thought I had better come round to the station and ask for you."

"You did the right thing, sir, absolutely the right thing. What I'm going to do now is to ask you to make a formal statement about what you've just told me — times, circumstances, descriptions — as detailed as you can make it." He pushed his chair back from the table. "Just put down everything as closely as you can remember it and then hopefully we won't have to trouble you again."

Pickering glowed. "Oh, thank you, that

would be a relief! One begins to feel so guilty . . ."

"Not to worry." He stood up. "Just put down every detail you can remember."

"I will, I will. I remember both of them were carrying hold-alls of some kind. They looked heavy. And the older one had some kind of folder or briefcase under her arm."

Simpson looked at him with love. "Would you fancy a cup of tea, sir, or coffee? We could run to a bun."

They parked outside Mr. Sobieski's house. A stonily chastened Blane enquired at houses on one side of it and Simpson himself on the other, as to whether two women carrying hold-alls had called at any of them on the afternoon in question, now some five weeks before. No one had.

Telling Blane to wait in the car, Simpson rang Sobieski's bell, noting the bare space where once "Frimwell" had been shakily printed. Sobieski opened the door; he seemed a little older but as though he were subsiding into a natural state rather than that of decay. He led Simpson courteously into his room, where the small votive light burned perpetually before a picture of the Sacred Heart. Refusing coffee, Simpson sat on one of the straight-backed chairs ranged round the central table, Sobieski opposite.

"I see you've not re-let the deceased's room yet, sir?"

"No. There was something about her death, so alone. . . . I feel perhaps there should be a period of mourning. I will see about it in a week or two." He smiled. "And perhaps it is not wrong that it remains for a while exactly as you found it?"

"What makes you think that, sir?"

Sobieski let a moment pass before replying. "I think there is something not quite right about Miss Frimwell's death, isn't that so? At first, yes — she's discovered, the constables come, the ambulance, it is natural causes, I think the phrase is, an old lady whose heart has simply stopped. But then, a week later, comes the CID and then the Fingerprints. You yourself and your impressive sergeant, who has paid some attention to poor Mr. Pickering, have continued over the weeks since. If this had indeed been a natural death I think, alas, it would have been forgotten long ago." He regarded Simpson quizzically, his hands clasped loosely between his knees.

An immense loneliness swept over Simpson. For years he had spoken to no one from his heart; not colleagues, who must not think him soft; not friends, for he had none outside his work; not girls, who were either thrilled or repelled by it, neither to his taste; not his father, grown old far away from him and from life. Not Hogarth, his superintendent, a hard man for whom black was black and there was precious little white; not Blane, with his inflexible attachment to his own prejudices; not, God knew, Janice, with her foolish, touching trust. He was a faceless man — or a masked man behind which was someone as alone as had been old Miss Frimwell, whom he had never known, yet who had come to represent for him the innocent, the vulnerable, the victim. He had become a policeman to protect such people, to stand between those who could not fight for themselves and punish those who preyed on them. It had not turned out like that; the wicked were not often punished, the victims were not often saved. In the seedy swamp of greed, violence and stupidity that made up Dave Simpson's world, he had lost himself.

He looked into Mr. Sobieski's face. It was not a mask as his own but the naked face of an old man who believed in God and therefore in Man. For some that was still possible.

"No," he said, "it wasn't a natural death. She was robbed and murdered."

"So." Mr. Sobieski crossed himself. "How?"

"I don't know. It might have been accidental, a robbery that went wrong. She was drugged and her heart gave out. Something was put in a drink, a cup of tea, whatever, to knock her out, that's what we think, and then they cleared the place of everything they could. There was no cash, jewellery, radio, clock . . ."

"Ah — poor Mr. Pickering and his clock!"

"They cleaned her out and left her. Washed and wiped everything, not a trace. Only her. Real pros."

"There are such. Not Mr. Pickering."

"Not Mr. Pickering." He allowed himself a smile. "But Mr. Pickering's come up with something. My sergeant's a bit over-conscientious but at least he shook the gentleman's memory up a bit. He's made a statement to the effect that on the relevant day, when the post-mortem tells us she died, he saw two women coming out of your garden gate. They were carrying hold-alls and walked away up the street away from him. He's given fair descriptions."

"Why only now?"

Simpson shrugged. "Things surface. What I'm here about now, sir, is to see if by any chance you can remember anything new along those lines. We know you weren't in on the afternoon in question. But did you ever see, anywhere about the neighbourhood, two women carrying hold-alls and some sort of briefcase, one of them tall, young, long hair, the other older, shortish, wearing a head scarf?"

"There are hundreds such."

"Too true. But loitering, perhaps, ringing doorbells and coming away, like as if they might be delivering freebies, junk mail?"

Mr. Sobieski was silent for a moment, his face slowly settling into an expression of pleasure. "Young man," he said at last, "coincidence is a strange thing. How often has one noticed, for no reason, some person in a shop or on a bus perhaps, of no significance at all, yet later that same day, in a different place, one sees them again? A one in a million chance, is it not, meaning quite nothing, but there it is, it has happened. So I think it may be now."

"You've seen them?"

"Not I. An old lady, a communicant at our church. After the Mass we gather together for coffee, cakes baked by our ladies — we are a strong community, bound by experiences as well as faith, growing old now, of course, but the young ones come and retain the spirit — they are Poles too, even though born here. We are a lesson in integration, don't you think, our own culture, our own language, our own church kept fully alive, yet all within the British fold, accepting the blessings of citizenship

— gratefully for the most part, if with some bitterness sometimes at promises betrayed. Uncle Joe — with trust you thought to draw the teeth of tigers!" He drifted away in thought, but sensed Simpson's impatience.

"You want facts, excuse me. This old lady, Mrs. Poniatowska, lives not far from here, in Marshall Street, a basement flat. She speaks hardly any English despite her many years here. Her husband was my friend, we were together in General Anders' army. He died a few years back. He always spoke for her, in the shops, on the buses and such, and their friends were all within the community, so she had no need to learn English, you see, and lacked confidence — a simple woman from a village near Lwow. He was able to get her out after the war, as were many with the help of your government. I tell you all this simply to explain why this old lady, over our coffee and cake, should tell me she was troubled that some official business had gone wrong, perhaps about her pension, because she had not been able to understand what was said by two women who called on her, official women with papers and cases. They spoke to her of Social Services, two words she does understand, but she could not understand the rest or they her, and they went away." He paused. "She wanted my advice, that I should find out if something was not in order for her — she lives always very much in fear now, being alone and not so young."

"And did you?"

"No. I thought it was of no importance, or that if it was, they could call again better prepared. I regret."

Simpson could feel the blood pumping up through his body. "When was this, sir?"

Sobieski thought. "I think it was the right time."

Mrs. Poniatowska was small and gnarled like the bark of an old tree. She moved laboriously through the jungle of her dark room like a beetle through the detritis of a wood, pushing and pulling, climbing and sinking, keeping up a sibilance of Polish to which Mr. Sobieski replied soothingly while Simpson stood wondering how long it would be before what little air there was in the basement room would be used up by the three of them. The room was heavily curtained, lit only by a weak-bulbed standard lamp in a corner and a votive light beneath a picture of Our Lady. Every surface was covered with lace doilies, yellowed and creased, and on most stood framed photographs of stiffly posed men and women, in uniform, in luxuriant peasant dress, in sober civilian costume of the turn of the century, and many, many pictures of the Pope. Waved to a dusty, doily-covered chair, he waited while the two old people trundled to and fro to settle at last with a doily-covered tray bearing coffee and almond biscuits set on the central table heaped with old Polish language newspapers and tracts, furry knitting on thick needles, spectacle cases and packets of sweets. For a moment they all sat silent, sipping and crunching, Mrs. Poniatowska regarding Simpson with the wary, testing stare of a survivor.

It was as Mr. Sobieski had said. Although she had not consulted him until two Sundays later, the women had called on her the day Miss Frimwell had died. She had not understood them, save for the words "pension" and "Social Services," not let them in. After mutual bafflement the one in the head scarf had said something impatient to the younger one and turned away. Mrs. Poniatowska had slammed and bolted the door and watched from behind the curtains as they went up the steps. The younger had worn jeans.

Simpson was revivified. The drive that had made him a policeman surged up again: the hunt, the capture, the demonstration of his own resources, cunning, brains. It was all coming together, his hunch had been right. Within an area of a few streets two women posing, it must be, as social workers had, on the relevant day, called on two old women. The Poniatowska and the Pickering descriptions tallied. The times checked — Poniatowska around mid-day, Pickering mid-afternoon. With Poniatowska it had been no dice; she had not let them in and they had gone away. At Sobieski's house they had better luck; they had bluffed their way, with their files and talk of pensions, into the confidence of that old lady, knocked her out with something in an oh-so-kindly-offered cup of tea, chatted her up with talk of benefits or irregularities or some rubbish of that kind until she fell asleep, then cleaned her out. And tidied up before they left, a professional job. A job that went wrong, like as not — murder, was not your con man's style, no need. An accident probably, bad luck. Especially for Miss Frimwell.

There must be others. Not other fatalities perhaps — although there could well be; it was mere chance that this one had landed up as a Suspicious Death. There must be other old women who had been conned, drugged, robbed, these things had a pattern. Confidence tricksters worked their scam till they were caught. They were not clever; cunning, resourceful, yes, but stupid in the end, seeing no further than the immediate gain, believing, in their contempt for ordinary people, that they were superior to them all.

They were not superior to Dave Simpson.

He could have kissed Mrs. Poniatowska — yes, even Pickering and his weirdo dolls — for now he had a case, a pattern, a jigsaw puzzle with only two pieces yet in place but they would be enough. He and the computers, the vast recorded web of police information that stretched across the country, all the huge organized power that had tempted him in and kept him there, a cog but a thinking cog, disillusioned and disheartened but still an officer of the law to catch criminals and protect the public. To be cleverer than the criminals and respected by the public.

He must be off his nut! How many people felt like that about the police force nowadays, public or coppers both? But he had once and did so now, as he helped the two old Poles into the car, Sobieski to interpret. Pickering's and Poniatowska's statements were the beginning of Dave Simpson's finest hour — he could feel it, he was fucking sure of it!

When their statements had been taken, the two of them sent home, the machinery of query, search and record set in motion, he went to see his boss.

Detective Superintendent Harry Hogarth sat behind his desk, big, bald and ugly as a Japanese wrestler, fingers laced over his belly.

He filled his suit as tightly as a sausage fills its skin, fat but hard fat, like suet. He listened, gooseberry eyes unblinkingly on Simpson, standing on the other side of the desk, asking permission to pursue the Suspicious Death.

"I thought that case was closed."

"No, sir. Shelved, more like. D.C. Blane's been keeping an eye."

Hogarth grunted. "Sharp lad, Blane. Make a good copper."

"Yes, sir."

"Twopenny-ha'penny case though, isn't it? Small-time thieving?"

"A fatality occurred, sir."

"Not titled, was she? Not an MP's granny? Not a pop star's favorite groupie?" Simpson said nothing. "Here's all this rising crime the papers tell us about . . ." He waved a massive hand towards his in-tray, "Muggings, break-ins, rapes, drug abuse. What's one old lady, like as not Accidental any road? And don't quote the Bible or poetry at me, Wally, I'm not in the mood."

He glared, but Simpson grinned back. He had worked under Hogarth long enough to know he had acquiesced. Partly from lack of interest — the case was a minor one; partly from duty — he was the hardest copper Simpson had come across, obsessive in his need to win against the villains; and partly because, for some odd reason, he had a soft spot for Simpson — perhaps the old bugger was lonely, regretted a son.

Hogarth hunched forward again, glowering up like an old bison. "You can have a week."

"Thank you, sir."

"But you can't have Blane."

"Right, sir." Good-oh!

"There's a manpower shortage, Wally. You're on your own."

"Okay, sir."

"At the end of the week, win or lose, back to the real world, understood?"

"Understood, sir."

"Right." He flapped a hand at him and Simpson moved to the door. As he opened it Hogarth made a joke. "The commissioner wouldn't like it, Wally."

Simpson grinned again. "The commssioner won't know," he said, and bounded back into the clatter of the outside office.

Thanks to the marvels of science, bit by bit the jigsaw took shape. From areas all over metropolitan London snippets of information blinked out from computers and from the meticulous records of local police stations. The complaints came in clusters, three or four in the same area over a period of several weeks, lists of articles stolen — all things mostly, like bits of jewellery, radios, sometimes as big as a fur or an oil painting; and cash, of course, always just after pension day. Always from old ladies. Always, as he mapped them, living in streets close to the High Street where would be the post office that paid out their pensions, and always near an Underground station. There were buses to reckon with, but Simpson fancied the Underground, quicker and more anonymous than waiting at a bus stop with a couple of hold-alls that might be noticed. They had begun in February of this year, at first across the river, then west, a few east, gradually drawing nearer his own patch. There had been five last month (probably more that were never reported), of whom the last was Miss Frimwell. Since then none. Coincidence? Or did they know she had died and taken fright?

He hoped not. He wanted to catch them.

He got in his car and drove to one of the addresses. The station report had been laconic, ending "Lady requests we ask Home Secretary for return of two Rockingham china figures 'after contents decoded.'"

Miss Greenham peeped round the basement door, which was on the chain. He showed his identity card. She opened the door and clutched his arm to pull him into the herbal-

298

scented darkness of the passage, re-chaining the door behind him.

"Don't speak," she whispered. "It's not safe."

She pushed him ahead of her past unseen obstacles into the back room, also in darkness save for the little light that came through the thin, drawn curtains. "Don't turn on the light," she said. "They can see in. I'm so relieved you've come."

She was a large woman who had crumpled, big shoulders and bosom bowed over wide hips and a stick, wild white hair thin at the roots, thick spectacles.

"Did you bring them?"

"Sorry?"

"My figures. Did you bring them?"

He smiled his most winning smile. "I'm Detective Inspector Simpson, CID, ma'am." He showed his card but she hardly looked at it, studying his face instead. "I'm investigating some recent cases of larceny and understand . . ."

"There's no need for all that nonsense," said Miss Greenham impatiently, "I understand perfectly well who you are, no need to put up a front. All I want to know is when my figures will be returned so that communication can be resumed."

"What figures are those, ma'am?"

"You know perfectly well. You had better sit down, I'm not able to use my legs as I used to, the danger has taken it out of me." She dropped into an armchair, very like the one in which Miss Frimwell had died save that it bulged and sagged more. She linked her hands over her stick and stared at him, breathing loudly.

He sat on a hard chair by the table, which was covered with newspapers and cuttings, a plate with the remains of jam on it, a dirty knife, margarine in a crusted paper, a mug with Charles and Di on it.

"No one from your people has been in touch since they called. It's very distressing. I fear they may have come to harm."

"The figures?"

"Them too. But mainly the two you sent. I've not seen them again and although I left a message at the police station, I've not had my figures back either. I'm afraid both they and your people may have been liquidated. They're ruthless, you know, quite ruthless."

The various "theys" were confusing. Simpson did his best. "I understand you called at the station quite soon after the — er — agents left with your property?"

"Oh no, of course not! I know better than that. It was quite a few weeks after because naturally I didn't want to alert them. I knew

300

they had to have time to decode and replan and return them to me. It was only when they weren't returned that I risked going to the police station to give them a little reminder. I can't get on with the messages, you see, the passing of information. I'm afraid to go out now, I might miss some message. And I really do fear they might do me some harm in the street, now they know I'm involved, and if the others are missing." She looked about her nervously, her white hair a mist in the gloom. "This is the only room I use now, the other's not safe. And even here they can see in from the garden, I have to keep the curtains tight drawn. Dear Mr. Akbar at the corner very kindly sends his son with what he thinks I might need in the way of provisions, and dear Corinda next door gets my pension. It's since your people left with my figures and they haven't come back that I'm sure they're on to me. I daren't go out."

"Did these people take anything else?" he asked gently.

"Oh yes, naturally. As cover, you see. I expected that. They took portable things, you know, to make it look right, little bits and pieces from the past."

"And cash?"

"Oh yes, they took the cash. I was a tiny bit surprised at that, I must say, but of course it all makes a convincing cover. I'm sure Mrs. Thatcher will see that it's repaid."

"I'm sure she will. It'll be on record somewhere, stuck in the files for a while, you know what government departments are like, ma'am."

A flash of vigour passed over her face. "Indeed I do. I was in the Ministry of Food all through the war."

"It would help me speed things up if I knew which these agents were. Did they give their names?"

"Of course. But I paid no attention because I knew they were false, naturally."

"What other cover story did they use?"

"From the Department of Social Services. Very clever, I thought it, social workers get in everything, no one gives them a thought. Black or white, they can pass through all doors, even Enoch Powell wouldn't suspect."

Simpson kept his head. "Could you describe them? Just in case they're from my own section?"

"Both were women, I thought that was clever, so plausible as social workers. Nicely turned out, quiet, middle-aged, just the kind to be convincing."

"Hair, clothes?"

"I don't notice that sort of thing. And I've always kept the curtains partly drawn, right from when I first knew. And since the figures haven't been returned I'm frightened to have them open at all. With silencers no one is safe." She sank back as though the chair would protect her.

"And the other one?"

"Younger. Tall. Not at all memorable — again, that's so clever, isn't it? Had her hair hanging down like they did a few years ago, so unbecoming except on really young girls. Those dear blacks are so lucky, never any problem with their kind of hair, so uncomplicated."

"Did they stay long?"

"Just long enough for a chat and a cup of tea. The young one very kindly made it while I told the older one all about my work and my suspicions and how I knew the IRA had come into it now, as well as the KGB. Naturally she didn't reveal anything about her side of it, but I told her all I knew. She was very understanding."

"And when did they leave?"

For the first time Miss Greenham's tension eased a little and she almost smiled. "Believe it or not, I fell asleep. It was the relief, you know, of them having made contact and listened to all my information. I fell asleep in this very chair and when I woke up they'd gone."

"And so had your things?"

"Well naturally. After all, that's what they came for, wasn't it?"

Simpson did not waste time wondering why he was so angry, so determined to find and stop these petty predators of the old and weak. There were plenty of worse crimes, more cruel villains. There was no violence here; even Miss Frimwell's death had been peaceful, almost certainly an accident. But for the technical need for a post-mortem, it would have been accepted as a natural death. But how many other old people might there have been, eased out of life a week, a month, a year too early, denuded of the small possessions that made up their being and that there was no one else to miss? How many others were left bewildered and afraid? In holes and burrows all over England old men and women hung on, bravely or bad-temperedly, drunk or sober, mad or sane, but entitled to life as long as it lasted, buttressed by their treasures, the objects that affirmed they had been young, had loved and been loved, worked, had skills, counted for something. Robbing them was a kind of murder, tricking them out of their past, a contempt of dignity. It was the contempt that enraged Simpson.

He visited all the complainants in his patch

(they were not many), wary of poaching on police divisions outside his own, much as he wanted to. The picture was always the same: two social workers, one middle-aged, one younger; the promise of extra benefits, the making of tea, the sleep, the awakening to find them gone and the realisation, perhaps not for days, that treasures and cash had gone too. The puzzlement, the shame, the indignation; worst of all, the humiliation of having been fooled. Old people's confidence grew weaker as their years advanced; to be conned like this made them feel they were no longer fit to cope. None of the possessions had ever been returned; details of some (those few that had been reported) lay in police records, but the objects themselves were too small or too anonymous ever to be tracked down. They were gone, taking lives with them — especially Miss Frimwell's.

He had interviewed officials at the local DHSS; no one from their department had been engaged on any such visits, no such extra benefits existed; no such two women as described were on their staff, no Mrs. Black, no Mary. The women he was after were cold-blooded tricksters.

A frustrated anger filled him. He had only a week, less now. For the first time he wished Jan knew his profession; she would not be much good, for she was not exactly a great intellect, but she would listen unquestioningly, and verbalising it to her would be helpful. To be a copper's girl you had to be special, and Jan was special because she asked no questions — he sometimes wondered if she was quite all there. But devotion is addictive. He had not been loved much since be grew up, and Jan's devotion aroused in him a protectiveness not altogether different from what he felt for those duped old women — *his* old women.

But Jan's subservience irritated him sometimes, especially when frustration seethed within him as it did now, and he found it hard to sit quietly on the sofa in Jan's room, watching the antics of the Two Ronnies on the television set he had rented for her — he had helped her out with quite a few things like that since her auntie left, for he knew she was a bit strapped for cash left on her own. True, she worked four days a week now at Continental Delicacies (black economy, he didn't want to know) and he intended she should get a proper job, pay insurance and be legitimate before much longer. Tidied up.

There must be something more he could do to track those con women down, but he could not think of it. He watched but did not see the screen in front of him, was hardly conscious of his arm around Jan, her head on his shoulder. He would not stay tonight; she had her period anyway, but he was not in the mood for sex. He should be out, asking questions, searching records, all the things he had already done with no result. But would do again.

There must be something, somewhere.

"You're ever so quiet, Dave."

"I'm okay."

"Will you stay tonight?"

"Not tonight. I'll be off soon."

"Oh, Dave." He knew she was hurt, believing he would not stay because they could not make love. In a way it was true, but her assumption irritated him; she put no value on herself. He gave her a squeeze and she at once put up her hand and turned his face to her, running her hand behind his head and kissing him deeply. A slight fire flickered in him but he pulled away, saying, "Hey-ey, cool it!" The tab of the zipper on his track suit caught in the chain of the locket she wore round her neck and had to be disentangled. Freed, he got up impatiently. "Coffee?"

"I'll do it."

"*I'll* do it!" He went and plugged in the kettle, rinsing the two dirty mugs that had stood on the floor beside the settee, spooned in the instant. The Two Ronnies came to an end, the nine o'clock news trumpeted on.

The Commons — "D'you reckon Mrs. Thatcher uses a tint?"; The Middle East — "You'd think they'd get tired of it"; a black statesman — "Isn't he shiny"; a Trades Union leader — "Ugh, look at his teeth!"; a police commissioner defending his force for the escape from custody of a resourceful robber — "Who does he think he's fooling?"

"What d'you mean?"

"Well, you know — it must've been a bent copper or something."

"Crap."

"But everyone knows there's bent coppers, Dave."

"Yeah, yeah, some. But we're some of us good guys. It gets up my nose people pissing on the police all the time. They should try the job."

Sipping the coffee, idly watching the rest of the news, he did not notice she had become as still as a rabbit in an open field; that she made no comment on the Princess of Wales visiting a nursery school; that when he switched off the set and said he was going she rose and stood silently while he shrugged on his anorak and that when he put his arm round her and kissed her cheek she did not respond but simply stared at him with eyes that seemed to be larger than usual. Vaguely he supposed she was feeling rough with her period, but by the time he was down the front steps and getting into his car he was back with Miss Frimwell.

Janice heard the door close behind him, his footsteps quick down the steps, the car driving away. She sat down on the settee again, the television screen blank before her. She had heard him, hadn't she? He had said, "We're some of us good guys." Not "*They're* some of them good guys," but "we're" — we. He was.

It all made sense. He wouldn't tell her, would he, because they never did, they were too careful. But it made sense. The shift work, the irregular hours, the why he never really told her anything, not things about his job, not where he worked, not where he lived. A civil servant. Well, you could call it that. It was she, wasn't it, who had somehow made out it was the post office. He'd never said yes or no. He'd never said anything. And she'd never asked because she was afraid to lose him.

She sat on the lumpy cushions of the sofa and tears began to roll out of her eyes and down her cheeks. They ran down her neck and into the top of her sweater and she wiped them away with the back of her hand. He would never, ever, move in with her or she with him. No wonder he'd never even let her know where he lived — in a police house, most likely, sharing with another cop or even a woman policeman. No wonder she never met his friends or went with him in a group. No wonder he never let her know anything about him.

He was a cop.

Here panic set in. She got up and began to walk about the room sobbing, leaning against the wall, then striking out again, wheeling to and fro between the shabby furnishings. He was a cop! What had she told him, what had she let fall? Nothing, surely, for when Grace had still been with her she had been too disciplined to do anything but lie. And since Grace left there had been nothing to hide, she had lived as best she could on her supplementary and Mr. Theodore's wages — she saw now why Dave had been so keen on her getting a job; he must have guessed she was on the fiddle and wanted her off it because he was the law. But he'd not grassed on her, had he, because he loved her. Didn't he? Didn't he love her, feel something more for her than all them others, all them pigs . . . ?

She lay down on the bed and let the tears run down the side of her face, into her ears, into the pillow. She had lost him, and with him her last faint hold on hope. Tears dissolved her. Quite soon she plunged into sleep.

* * *

She got herself to work next day — it was Wednesday, early closing, Continental Delicacies fairly quiet with only a few OAPs dithering about over the deep freeze and girls with kids in push-chairs stocking up on crisps and biscuits. Mr. Theodore was in one of his rages, a huge black-browed volcano, because a batch of yoghurt had gone past their sell-by date, his son-in-law Costa's fault, for he had allowed them to stay at the back of the cold cabinet to be overlaid by newer stock. Costa sat behind the till in silence as Mr. Theodore banged and cursed out of sight in the stockroom, gazing with dark Byzantine eyes at the customers and their proffered money and at Janice price-stamping tins of cat food.

Janice was hardly conscious. When she had woken up that morning she had been convinced she had got it wrong; Dave had not said that, she had misheard him, of course he wasn't a cop, everything was okay. But as she slopped about getting her breakfast, doing her face, despair had welled over her. She had not been mistaken, it all made sense. She went to work like a zombie, incapable of any kind of thought save misery.

When the shop closed at one o'clock she went straight home. She found Grace there, sorting through a quantity of silver and other

311

objects which she had laid out on the bed.

Grace looked up with a smile. "Oh hullo, Jan. I thought you might be back. Well, come in, girl, don't just stand there." She turned back to the bed and continued to sort spoons and forks into different sizes, wrapping six of each briskly in newspaper.

"Where've you been?" Janice asked faintly.

"That'd be telling. Let's say I had something good lined up but it didn't work out. I've not done too badly, though." She surveyed the loaded bed complacently. Beside it stood three handsome leather suitcases in various sizes, a shabbier plastic, zippered case and some John Lewis plastic carriers. "We haven't got any tissue paper, have we, or some little boxes? I don't want things to get all tangled up."

As though hypnotised, Janice came to the bed. It was covered with a variety of objects of the kind with which she had been familiar in the old working days, but far more of them and of much greater worth. As well as the loose cutlery, a flat mahogany case was open to show rows of mother-of-pearl-handled fruit knives and forks bedded in green baize compartments. There were three silver christening mugs and several silver ashtrays. Wrapped in a good silk scarf were several sets of china flowers. Other silk scarves, male and female, held a jumble of jewellery — gold chains, brooches, a set of pearl evening-dress studs and a gold fob watch. There were ivory brushes, a silver flask and cigar case; several silk blouses, a cashmere twin set. Up on the pillows was a gold brocade evening jacket with a white fox collar, and laid over the back of a chair a Persian lamb coat.

Bemusedly Janice asked, "How ever did you get all this stuff?"

"Well, I brought the cases too, didn't I — they're good solid leather, should fetch a bob or two. And I left most of my own old stuff there, only brought toilet things and that and just a few clothes, so I had my own old case as well. And the carriers. It was quite a job packing up, though, I can tell you." She began putting the wrapped cutlery into one of the plastic carriers. "Then I phoned up a mini to take me to King's Cross, and got a train from there."

"You never wrote, Grace."

"No, well, I didn't know where I was going to be, did I. Don't just stand there, dear, I want to get this small stuff wrapped up."

Automatically Janice obeyed her, wrapping the smaller objects in half-sheets of newspaper while Grace, remembering, went to the dressing-table and found handkerchiefs and a scarf or two among the muddle of

Jan's possessions. These she used for the jewellery.

"Thanks, dear. I don't want to hang about with the selling, not the small stuff."

"Why did you come back?"

"Well, it was convenient, wasn't it. I'd still got my key and I reckoned you'd still be here, knowing what a wet fish you are." She laughed indulgently. "And if you hadn't been, well, no harm done, was there."

Panic seized Jan and she stopped packing, staring at Grace in horror. "You're not stopping?"

"Just for a day or two, till I get most of this lot shifted. I'll go up the markets and round to old Feinstein this afternoon, then the furs and the bigger stuff I'll pack up in the cases and take round to never-you-mind tomorrow morning."

"You can't!"

"What d'you mean, can't? I'm here, aren't I?" She put the last piece into a John Lewis bag and hefted it to gauge its weight.

"You can't! Dave might come!"

"You still on with him, then? Well, he'll just have to lump it for once, your auntie's come back on a visit."

"Grace — he's a copper."

"What?" It was as though an iceberg had suddenly slid into the room, glassy, silent and motionless. The two women stared at one another across the strewn bed, statues. Grace's face drained white; then, as she took a step towards Janice, flushed crimson up to her dyed hair. "He's a what?"

"A copper." The words were whispered and Jan began to shake, stepping back from the bed and up against the wall, her face as white as Grace's had been.

"You been going with a copper?"

"I didn't know. He never said." She began to babble, feeling the wall behind her like a barrier rather than a support. "I never keew what he was. He was just a fella, he never said, I thought he was in the post office, working shifts and that. I never knew where he lived even, he never said."

"And you never asked."

"I didn't want to upset him."

Grace took a breath. Her colour had subsided and she stood menacingly still. "So how d'you know now?"

"He let it out. He didn't realise."

"When was this?"

"Last night."

"Right." She moved into action, her face hard as stone. "Get packed."

"What?"

"Get packed." She heaved the leather suitcases up on to the bed and began stuffing first the blouses and then the remaining small objects in among them.

"No!"

"I'm not leaving you behind to shop me soon as he looks at you."

"He doesn't know — not nothing!"

"He soon will, the state you're in."

"No, he won't! He thinks I'm straight. I've got a job, I'm going to get insurance."

"And you think that'll work? You think you'll be O.K. and nice and cosy tucked up in bed with a copper? Use your head, girl. How long d'you think it'll be before you get nervous, let something out, think he's on to you? How long before he *is* on to you, the closer you get? No, thank you very much! It's not what I'd intended, but there's no help for it. You're coming with me."

"No!" She began to cry, standing up against the wall with her hands and her hair hanging down, a thin pale woman of nearly thirty from whom the transient bloom of the last few weeks had been drenched away in an instant.

Grace glanced at her with contempt, busy wrapping and folding; then her gaze sharpened and her hands stilled for a moment. "And what's that round your neck?" Janice's hand went up to the locket on its chain. "That's what you pinched from that old

316

biddy who sussed us out weeks ago, isn't it? You silly bloody bitch, I told you to get rid of it, didn't I? Didn't I?" She came round the bed and took Janice by the arms, shaking her so that her head bumped against the wall. Grace's face was red, her eyes bright with fury. "I *told* you. I *told* you! Never keep nothing traceable, I've told you. There's lists, there's computers, they link up with everything. That bit of rubbish round your neck's on a list somewhere and you say your man's a cop!" She shoved her away and Janice collapsed on to the bed, her sodden hair hiding her face.

Grace looked at her coldly. "When's he coming back?"

"I don't know."

"Right. We have to be out of here inside the hour, then. It's a pity I can't shift some of this stuff before we go, as intended, but we'll just have to take as much as we can and try our luck up north. Just take what you need of your own stuff, underwear and that, and leave the rest. We can easy get some new when we're settled."

She turned away. On top of the wardrobe were two cheap suitcases belonging to Janice and these she took down and banged on to the bed. She pulled open the drawers of the dressing-table. "There," she said, "get packed."

"I can't!"

"Get moving."

This was not what Grace had planned. She had acquired more from the Robinsons' flat than she ever had before, ransacking the place while the old cow lay snoring in her chair after her elevenses, the Bovril laced with the usual sherry and the unusual residue of the pills Grace had brought with her when she abandoned Janice. She had crushed the whole lot up on the Robinsons' breadboard after Conroy left for business that morning and stirred it all into his mother's mid-morning drink. It had not taken long for her to go off, snorting and sagging in her chair like some disgusting old walrus. Grace had gone swiftly round the flat, taking everything she could pack into the suitcases and carrier-bags, stuffing the cash into her handbag — there had been several hundred pounds hardly hidden here and there. She had turned Conroy's chest of drawers out on to the floor and thrown his suits off their hangers, for she knew how he hated disorder; and coldly, after she had packed up his valuables, she had unlocked the deed box and torn his divorce papers and the photograph of Carole

318

June in half — the divorce papers were quite tough.

She had packed everything (leaving her own clothes, chain-store stuff, anonymous), put on Mrs. Robinson's Persian lamb coat, rung for a mini-cab; then she went back into the hot, darkly curtained lounge to take a last look at the old cow unconscious in her chair. She would have liked to take the rings from the old cow's fingers but did not think she could risk tugging them over the swollen knuckles. After a moment's thought she had smashed the glass of the big picture-frame that held half a dozen studio photographs of Marion Conroy in costume which hung over the mantelpiece. Then she had taken the luggage quietly out of the apartment block to wait in its gateway for the cab; there were few people about at that time of the day. Conroy would not be back till late that evening — she had chosen a Wednesday on purpose. And she really did not care what he might find on his return, nor how Mrs. Robinson would survive her eventual waking — if she did wake.

She had come back to Jan's place because, as she had said, it was convenient. She had a key still, she knew the various "outlets" in the neighbourhood where she could sell her loot and no questions asked. Then she had intended to be on her way to the Midlands somewhere, Birmingham perhaps, with or without Janice — probably without. Just Number One.

Janice had stopped crying but lay hunched up on the pillows, her face hidden. Grace moved into the outer half of the room and drew the curtains. "Get hold of yourself, girl. I'll make us a cup of tea."

Jan sat up, pushing the hair off her face. "I love him, Grace!"

"Tough luck."

"We was going to get married."

"To a copper? Pull the other one, dear."

"I can't leave him, Grace. I'll die."

"No, you won't, you'll end up in stir again. If that's what you want, right." Deftly getting mugs and tea-bags, Grace spoke drily: "How long d'you think it'll be before he's on to you? And what d'you think he'll do then — give you a kiss and say you've been a naughty girl, don't do it again? He's the fuzz, Jan, it's his job! He'll put you away soon as he's got the evidence — and some of that's hanging round your neck, you silly cow, isn't it?" Janice gave a sob. "In any case, that's no good to me. Soon as he was on to you, he'd be on to me. You might not know just where I'd gone but you know a damn sight too much about me to be left on your own down here and let your copper follow me up. No, thank you very much, Jan, you're best off with me." She poured the boiling water on to the tea-bags and brought the mugs to the table. "Get your skates on now. We haven't got all day."

10

Detective Inspector Dave "Wally" Simpson sat with his head in his hands while across the desk Detective Superintendent Harry Hogarth regarded him dispassionately, leaning back in his chair so that his hard flesh bulged tightly within his clothes, his hands pressed flat on the blotter on which lay a letter. No emotion disturbed his expression but in his eyes, small in his large face like those of some sagacious hog, there could have been a glint of something very like affection.

After a while he said, "I won't accept it, Wally."

"You have to. I've made a right ballsup."

"That's right."

"I'm a rotten copper."

"You're a silly fart."

Simpson wiped his hand over his eyes; he was not crying but he felt as though he were. His face was haggard, sweaty, and he looked up at Hogarth without hope.

He had gone to Jan's place that evening,

half-past nine, something like that; used his key as usual; found the room empty. Wardrobe and drawers open, half her clothes gone or dropped on the rumpled bed among sheets of newspaper, crumpled and of past dates. From the dressing-table most of her make-up gone, only a litter of powder, lipstick smudges, tissues.

Two mugs with tea-bags in them on the table. Two cigarette stubs squashed in a saucer; Jan did not smoke.

Bewildered, alarmed, alerted, he had gone back into the bedroom half of the room and stood there, looking. His heart had begun to beat more quickly, more loudly, as his instincts and his training began to work. As carefully as possible he had searched further. In the bottom of the wardrobe, stuffed into a John Lewis plastic bag, he had found a 1920s style brocade jacket with a white fox collar and caught in its hairs a pair of artificial pearl earrings. There was a real silk square smelling of mothballs half hidden under the bed. On the bedside table still stood his own noisy alarm clock which she always wound but never turned on, and under it a scrap torn from one of the strewn sheets of newspaper — a white piece, part of a display advertisement probably. On the white part she had scrawled, it looked like in eyebrow pencil, "I love you, Dave."

With dread, he had gone down to the basement where an aged Sikh, suffused with the fumes of curry, listened gravely to him, and from between impeccable turban and frothing beard, declared he had seen nothing, knew nothing, did not care. Houses on either side were empty or unobservant, save for one old man who thought be remembered a taxi arriving — don't often see taxis round here — while he was shaving in the window to get the light, see, although his stubble seemed to disprove that. A lot of luggage had come out of the taxi and gone in next door, he'd noticed that — lunchtime it must have been, he liked to shave before going out for his half-pint lunchtime. A woman, he thought, middle-aged. Looked like the one he used to see next door, hadn't seen for a while. Couldn't be sure, though. Used to go around with a younger one, long hair. She'd been there still, he'd seen her sometimes, all tarted up. Hadn't seen nothing more, he'd gone out, hadn't he, down to the Feathers, had a kip when he got back. Sorry, guv.

Auntie. Glimpsed once weeks ago, when he'd been checking where Jan lived, before he and she got serious and Auntie left. The two social workers, described. The locket . . .

Then back to the station, heart cold, and the check through the records of stolen property. It was there, a complaint from an OAP two months back, with other things. Jan had always worn it, even in bed, thought it turned him on, just the locket and nothing else. . . . Maybe it had.

"You're a silly fart, son," Hogarth repeated, "but you're a good copper. You have to be, I picked you. I trained you up, Wally, and that's enough."

"Not for me, not now."

"It is for me, and I'm the one that counts. Who's on this with you?"

"No one. You took Blane off."

"And I'm taking you off too. You can have a nice quiet stint in Records or somewhere, get yourself sorted out. Still got the key, have you?"

Simpson felt in his pocket and laid it on the blotter, next to his resignation letter. Hogarth picked it up, took a grubby handkerchief from his pocket and gave the key a good rub. Replacing it on the blotter, he took up the letter and tore it slowly into several pieces, dropping them into the wastepaper bin.

"Acting on information received," he said, poker-faced, "some of my lads can call at that address and have a nice look-round. I daresay there'll be some useful dabs about if one or other of the girls has got form, as seems highly probable."

"There'll be mine too."

"Yes, well — they'll be eliminated, won't they. Then there's some little bits and pieces lying about, from what you tell me — that brocade jacket in the wardrobe sounds interesting. Too big to pack in a hurry, I shouldn't wonder, and a garment someone's bound to identify. Likely some other Divs had got complaints filed away somewhere too, little things gone missing here and there, there'll be a record somewhere. Who knows, some other old biddy may have been done the same way while we've been sitting here, and been reported. And we've got good photofits. Those two old ladies you chased up aren't so batty as not to have had a good look. We could mock up an identikit from Greenham alone, we don't hardly have to bring you into it."

"But . . ."

Hogarth held up a hand. "I run this section, son. I don't give a tuppeny fuck what you or anyone else wants. I know my lads and they get results and that's all I'm bothered about. You're a good copper, Wally, and you're one of mine. Now piss off."

Simpson stood up. He felt an old, old man.

He felt disgust at his own blindness, at being deceived; and more than that, a deep mourning sadness — for loss, for betrayal, for rottenness, for hope. He had loved her — nearly. She had loved him, he knew. Honest, they might have made it together: security for him, salvation for her. His wounds were not deep, though they throbbed. She might die of hers, in the end.

Like Miss Frimwell.

Hogarth watched him go. "Chances are we'll catch them, Wally. Sooner or later."

"I know," said Simpson, and left the room, shutting the door quietly behind him.

THORNDIKE-MAGNA hopes you have enjoyed this Large Print book. All our Large Print titles are designed for easy reading, and all our books are made to last. Other Thorndike Press or Magna Print books are available at your library, through selected bookstores, or directly from the publishers. For more information about current and upcoming titles, please call or mail your name and address to:

THORNDIKE PRESS
P.O. Box 159
Thorndike, Maine 04986
(800) 223-6121
(207) 948-2962 (in Maine and Canada call collect)

or in the United Kingdom:

MAGNA PRINT BOOKS
Long Preston, Near Skipton
North Yorkshire,
England BD23 4ND
(07294) 225

There is no obligation, of course.